Some
of the
Whole Truth

By
Mark Sproule-Jones

Strategic Book Publishing and Rights Co.

Strategic Book Publishing and Rights Co.
12620 FM 1960, Suite A4-507
Houston TX 77065
www.sbpra.com

ISBN: 978-1-62857-879-9

Dedicated to
Megan and Amy

Preface

This is a fast-paced novel about duplicity, cunning and sex in Canadian politics. It is almost a first for novels set in Canada. It is about real world politics in Ottawa and Washington, with the major characters being the prime minister, his wife and chief advisors, as well as the American president and the secretary of state, who is also his mistress. Canadian novels love to skirt around the seamy aspects of Canadian politics, preferring tales of social issues and moral dilemmas. This novel differs in that it is influenced by the tone of John le Carre's early books about cold war spying in Britain, while retaining a distinct Canadian cultural feel.

It is a short novel, with constant changes of scene in and between chapters. Films and television shows have changed presentation methods in the last decade. Scenes last about four seconds unlike in previous years when settings and conversations could last many minutes. Novels have never really copied the new media techniques. While many authors change the pacing in a novel by using dialogue to speed up and situational descriptions to slow down, this book uses rapid sequencing of parallel story lines to keep the reader fully absorbed. This newer method may presage comparable changes in the e-book age.

The author is a professor emeritus of political science and has published 12 books of non-fiction and 70+ academic articles. He uses his expertise to accurately depict the nature of prime ministerial and Cabinet decision making, of the bureaucratic free enterprise practised by security forces like the Royal Canadian Mounted Police (RCMP) and the Central Intelligence Agency (CIA), and of the electoral bases of politicians brought up and tutored in places like Victoria, Toronto, Newark and Terre Haute. The works of C.P. Snow act as a very approximate guide.

Finally, there are three women in this story who play key roles in a world of clever, strategic and ruthless men. One is the prime minister's wife, a tough matron who uses pillow talk to get her way. A second is a younger "first-term" Member of Parliament from Burnaby, British Columbia, who crosses the floor to join the governing party in Parliament. She admits that lust and power are motivators and the prime minister the target. The third is a street-wise politician from New Jersey, formerly a governor and now secretary of state, whose modus operandi is distrust all rivals for influence in DC.

Mark Sproule-Jones,
Burlington, Ontario
November 2013

Table of Contents

Chapter One:
Playing with Fire

He made a point of going to the Cabinet room early—well, about an hour early, roughly half-past eight—and with strict orders to the attending commissioner to keep all others out, including his wife, until 9:25 am.

He would sit in his chair and swivel it around to see out of the windows to his left. He used to conjure new and different places to seat his colleagues. He had offended protocol, deliberately, at his first Cabinet meeting. He liked to face his allies, place the more thoughtful next to him and always put the hostile ones at the corners unless it seemed they might collude. It made sense to move everybody at different meetings. It kept discussions lively and shuffled the hostile and admiring glances.

He reserved time at these solitary sojourns for reading or re-reading the executive summaries of briefs delivered the day previous, with luck before 7 pm. A night's sleep, good or otherwise, gave his subconscious the room and time to spell out the pros and cons and whether he really cared about the conclusions. Many affairs of the state could wait and mature, he discovered, like the Croft's port he enjoyed sipping late at night.

At about 9:25 am the ministers would dribble in, always frantically preceded by the Clerk and his crew of scribblers and laptop merchants. You could never count on ministers to remember to bring their briefs. Too busy could be a legitimate excuse. The smile on the House Leader's face betrayed some good news, and it now would set the tone for the rest of the group.

He didn't like to fill the seats around the walls with every aspiring deputy minister, let alone ministers of the state. He had prided himself on getting good products from working committees, and their written-only products could easily be garnished by the comments of attending ministers.

Today's welcoming introductions were quickly followed by the Prime Minister's request for an agenda change to allow the House Leader, Gilles, to make an announcement. Anne Barnaby, the NDP critic for social policy and housing, had agreed to cross the floor of the House. It increased the Prime Minister's majority to twenty-four but more importantly it would give him some numerical strength in Metro Vancouver, a city long lost to those in $1,000 suits.

The main items on the agenda today were economic. That meant a long review of the state of the national economy, of particular issues like commodity prices and of prospects for worldwide markets and economics. This meant a dry but necessary twenty-minute introduction by John Bradshaw, his Minister of Finance, followed (he would insist) by comments first from the Minister of National Revenue on revenue projections. He could always come back another time to expenditure items, for these were never packageable enough for orderly deliberations by the twenty-six sitting around the table.

As John advanced his theses and comments, Arthur Jones, the PM, liked to lean back in his chair and reflect on the spirit of these meetings. There was a liturgy to them, familiar and warming. With luck he would avoid the sermon and have colleagues murmur agreements and otherwise in the more hallowed tones of august priests. This was really where he was meant to be.

There were times in his past at both federal and provincial levels when the agenda unravelled. Comments elicited more and more outrageous ones, and Arthur would essentially give up refereeing, in the hope that exhaustion would overtake the speakers. Rarely did it do so. His colleagues would often begin to resemble squabbles of seagulls on a sandy beach, flying and hopping at crumbs of food, with piercing squawks and rising tempers. He felt in time that good organisation, control of the agenda, prior review of contentious issues could keep things civil. The drivers of war were best kept to times of acknowledged battles.

The discussion of John's brief was short and desultory. He had not given them much in the way of conclusions other than the usual "close monitoring calls" especially over grain prices. Concerns about softwood lumber were never handled well at this level, and were best sent to the resources and environment committee after due consideration by the MNR Minister (Minister of Natural Resources). They might die there, as Jimmy, the cautious Albertan minister, was more a Scottish Presbyterian cleric in temperament than an impulsive intervener into provincial interests. Arthur was glad this meeting was going to finish before noon. Now he needed to let the Cabinet in on some "secrets."

Secrets they were not to some. He had already discussed the issues with Raj (his Minister of Foreign Affairs), Gilles and John, Mario (his Deputy Prime Minister from Montreal) and some of his Prime Minister's Office (PMO) staff. All loyal men. Why no women?—he must look into that, he mused.

Here it goes, he thought. "New business. I must say a few words. We have discovered that the Americans, we believe in the Pentagon, have hacked into our deepest core of e-transmissions, past the two firewalls and through to my inner office. We can't figure out why. We don't leak their confidences. We support them on foreign affairs almost to the point of electoral embarrassment."

He felt it best to end there, but added that the Cabinet committee on foreign affairs, defence and security would meet that afternoon. He would be there for most of the meeting, and Raj would brief him on the full discussion later that evening. Arthur would be inviting a few over to Sussex Drive after dinner, but he kept that quiet in case they all wanted to attend.

The Prime Minister told Cabinet that they should keep these developments secret for now. He knew this was the best way to prompt orderly leaks of government business. There were always one or two ministers who owed a parliamentary correspondent a favour. He didn't expect a television discussion tonight. Too many layers of approvals and arse-kissing at the CBC, and CTV people never liked working after 5 pm. No, it would run in Saturday's *Globe* and *Mail* or the TORSTAR chain, and the endless pages of editorials would begin next week.

For the time being, he needed to discover what the Yankees were up to. At noonish he escaped further questions, thanks to a thirty-minute meeting with Anne Barnaby before a lunch with Stephen, his Chief of Staff. With luck he might get forty winks before his intensive committee discussion.

Anne was refreshing—perpetually optimistic, a go-getter, and always with a big smile. He enjoyed her company. He had, in fact, taught her in third-year law courses not too many years ago. A good, viable A- student with strong convictions about helping the marginalized. He had two agenda items for her to think and then worry about. The issues had been passing comments in his manifestos but needed action now in order to mature in concept and start in implementation before the next election. The items involved investing or pushing for hospices for Canada's growing elderly population. Lots of ideas there. The other was, he knew, close to her heart. It was developing a new Canada Mortgage and Housing Corporation push into bachelor apartments in central cities, for the burgeoning numbers of single men and women. That issue required delicate provincial negotiations. Anne would be up for it.

Arthur outlined those priorities to her after the usual pleasantries and thanks for her courage to switch allegiances. He said that he required some weeks to orchestrate a smooth reshuffle of Cabinet. The current minister of state for housing needed to maintain face, stay loyal and embrace a different challenge more suited to her suite of skills, which lacked any taste and energy for infighting with entrenched "we know best" bureaucrats.

* * *

When Raj arrived after dinner, he was in quite a flap. Everyone around the sub-committee table had different prescriptions for dealing with the issue, but Raj impressed on them that any decision had to involve the PM directly. By now the White House would have realised that their strategy or blunder would be known in Canada's top circles. They would be expecting the Prime Minister to respond personally, perhaps by phone, to the President himself. Now all kinds of possibilities could open up.

Gilles joined the group at about 7:15 pm, moaning about slow traffic meandering past the Christmas lights and other decorations. It was also never easy to speed past the American Embassy. Gilles was quite delightful in moments of crisis—an ebullient poker player with a big smile and bigger tummy upon which often sat a pair of large brown hands.

Arthur opened the discussion by confirming what Raj already knew. Canada's Ambassador had no information to share. The Prime Minister asked Raj to have his deputy minister contact the American Embassy to tell the US Ambassador that Canada's defence review was at its midpoint, and ask if the Ambassador would prefer to hear the conclusions confidentially before a final draft was prepared. It was always useful to put such people in a quandary. The Ambassador would know about the review but wouldn't be aware that it was close to conclusion. Arthur encouraged Raj's deputy minister to wonder aloud to the US Ambassador if Canada's own Ambassador in Washington might keep the Secretary of State more up to date. Ambassadors hated being out of the loop—any loop!

While Raj phoned his deputy, Arthur asked Gilles for an update on the state of play of Canada's security forces based in DC. Did the committee discuss their role this afternoon? Gilles murmured some words about the country's skeleton resources in eavesdropping, forgetting perhaps that the Department of National Defence (DND) had its own parallel systems to those of the Canadian Security Intelligence Service (CSIS).

When Raj returned, the Prime Minister began a discussion on how to proceed firmly and with strategic guile. He felt it might be useful to create some allies overseas on this issue. The Brits would join anything perfidious, but they were unreliable where the Americans were concerned. France was too devious. Israel offered the best choice—always strategic, suspicious and ready for mixed strategy games. The PM offered to handle the issue directly with their Prime Minister tomorrow; he would outline the threat to Canada's interests if it became merely a client state of the US. That would resonate with them.

All present agreed that Raj should ask the US Ambassador for a meeting, but not too early in the day. Let him fester. Raj would also recall our UN Ambassador from New York even though he was a appointee of limited guile. The symbolism would surprise the US Secretary of State and divert some attention from other strategies. The object was to create so much traffic of a difficult nature on the eavesdroppers that consequences of any actions by them would escalate with uncertainties.

* * *

No one thought the Israeli PM would be surprised by Arthur's revelations. Better still he was quite bemused and offered his help with some alacrity. He was tired of America's penchant for supporting everyone involved with Palestine. Win—win—win and more seemed to be their goal. Here was a chance to remind the US of a real Middle Eastern power.

He agreed to cooperate in devising a strategy to obtain oblique entry into the Pentagon's computer core. Israel had some codes that took them past initial firewalls, ostensibly in case Hamas proved belligerent inside towns like Tel Aviv or Jerusalem. Once inside, Canada would supply some dummy information about security risks within the defence establishments of a number of NATO countries. The President loved it; the plan was a brilliant practical joke..

The phone call was made from Arthur's parliamentary office but patched through to that of the defence minister. No office seemed fully secure now. The Department of National Defence was occasionally in contact with Israel and, even if the Americans twigged to the leaks, they would be confused and surprised by these developments.

The ministers of defence and national security were both given authority to get their hackers working on the indirect line through Israel and the direct line to the White House.

So, with the elements of "create the confusion" in place, it was time to launch Canada's offensive retaliation. Arthur would call the President tonight. The President hated to be reached on Air Force One. It was supposedly his secure love nest in the sky.

Chapter Two:
Keeping It Alight

Barry Evans was one of those ebullient, friendly politicians who characterized much of Indiana's body politic. The smile was always broad, the body language attentive and only occasionally did his blue eyes betray another agenda. Born in the Corn Belt east of Fort Wayne, he had honed his political skills in the United Automobile Workers, a union that still revered Walter Reuther and the Congress of Industrial Organizations. Automobile workers used to believe in their superior values prior to the Toyota invasion. Barry never fell into that trap. The Indiana Democratic Party rested on two foundations: the United Automobile Workers and the United Steelworkers. Neither could be alienated, at least not in state-wide elections. And neither could afford to ignore the importance of Japanese-owned automobile companies and their thousands of nonunionized employees in Indiana and other states.

The Prime Minister knew all this about President Evans. But he only found out recently that Barry's zipper was never constantly vertical. Mutual friends in Indiana University Law School always spread malicious gossip, true or false. And CSIS loved nothing better than verifying the rumours of others. Unkind bureaucrats suggested that this was because they were too slow to find their own. Prime ministers needed to recognize when some gossip could be lost and others filed for future occasions. Barry's blue eyes might be a source of his undoing, so to speak.

Prime Minister Arthur Jones was not to play this trump card in his discussions with the President, at least for now. But he savoured the potential embarrassment of calling the President on a long-distance overnight flight to Canberra. People awakened from a sound

15

sleep, even a torrid sleep, rarely spoke with a clear mind. Might this prove to be a cute little trap for a sleepy president?

"Mr. President. I apologize for calling so late, but our government in Canada is perplexed and horrified by some news. Our communications systems into my office and that of our defence minister have, we think, been penetrated by some hackers from Russia. We think they are former KGB but are not sure. We fear our defence secrets and those we share with the US and other allies may be compromised. Can you help us? We need verification. We need dates of entry. We need any hackers' codes you could reveal. We then need you to help us communicate this disturbing event to NATO powers."

"Arthur, I'm pleased you called although tomorrow might have been a more pleasurable time. I am not aware of this Russian hacking threat. I'll put our people on it right away. It would be best if you postponed contacting our mutual allies. We need some good proof. Putin is very touchy about NATO and its organization."

"Can you direct your CIA people to link up with our CSIS group and work together to determine the plausible ways that our firewalls could have been broken? They have the resources and expertise to help our smaller group. And they might help us seal up our network holes."

"We would love to help, Arthur. Let me put my Secretary of State in charge of the next steps."

"That would be great, Barry. We have also put our ambassador in Washington on full alert. Give my best to Beryl the next time you see her in person."

Arthur hung up immediately. He waited for no pregnant pauses or stifled gasps. Secretary of State Beryl Rossini was a pawn for Barry Evans, a good blonde shag who liked to travel and could never embarrass him. Arthur just wanted Evans to know his secret was common knowledge in high diplomatic circles. En garde, Barry.

* * *

Raj felt that everyone was moving too quickly. He didn't really grumble about the chosen strategy, but he had serious concerns about its broader goal: letting Canada's allies know that the US could no longer be considered as trustworthy. "What would we get in return?" was his first comment. "Could the US just scramble our entire communication systems in retaliation?" was his second.

Arthur's response was "lots" and "no," respectively. What he proposed was to leak joint defence secrets through US government and WikiLeaks, which would create an image of the US as a destroyer of the secrets of allied sovereign nations. No friend to its friends, in other words. Canada would then have the space to rebuild its systems. As to the threat of US retaliation, the Americans already knew the important features of Canada's information technology infrastructure. Any further destruction would simply amplify the negative world image of the US. Raj smiled with some glee. He once revealed how much he hated Beryl Rossini, who had been overheard on several occasions calling him that "little Indian guy."

* * *

Arthur knew the afternoon would be more hectic than ever. By now he'd guessed that rumours were starting to spread around the Hill and offices in central Ottawa. He had needed to have his Chief of Staff reach the deputy minister of national defence and the director of CSIS to begin work. Raj had kept his deputy and the ambassador in DC more or less in the loop. Gilles had run some interference in caucus. But these starts could lead to expanded briefings in the civil service. Soon the press would amplify the gossip. Every executive-level bureaucrat felt that the required oath of secrecy could be trumped by a leak from an "unattributed source."

Soon the calls from Cabinet colleagues would start. Best to head them off. Gilles could handle the junior ministers. John, in Finance, Mario, in Montreal, and Tom, the Minister of National Defence, all needed first-hand briefings. Stephen would notify the Cabinet of emergency meetings scheduled for the day after tomorrow to allow the wanderers and travellers to get back to Ottawa as well as to give Arthur some extra breathing room. Graham, the Clerk of the Privy Council, was undoubtedly pissed off. He liked to think the Clerk was the pivot around which the federal government circled. Even after six months he still had not twigged to the fact that Arthur ran his deputy ministers through his own office.

* * *

Finally it was time to go home. One of the few perks that Arthur really enjoyed—and he rationalised his need for it too—was access to a limousine and driver. Sometimes an RCMP officer sat up front with the driver. Arthur always felt the Mountie's first priority would be to save the driver before glancing into the back seat.

Arthur hated driving in twilight and late evening in Ottawa. Bored young men traversed the town at self-destructive speeds. With a busy day gone and the anticipated, he didn't need more stress. And snowflakes were starting, always an ambiguous augur for Canadian prime ministers since Trudeau.

He looked forward to seeing Jane. He spent so much time dealing, if not wheeling, with people at work or on the phone that it was easy to forget his "primary relationship." It was lucky she enjoyed party politics; there was always a meeting, conference or a cabal to join and discuss and discuss and discuss. Bits and pieces did, of course, find their ways into public discourse, but much was essentially of therapeutic value to the party loyalists. Jane found it easier to relate to their BC riding activists than the flotsam around Parliament Hill. But she was alert to new ideas and new politics, and kept Arthur engaged with these when they squeezed out time together. It had been easier before the kids went to university. Now they knew long periods of loneliness even in the midst of crowds and partisans.

Arthur recognised the ending of their passions and felt a little envious of Barry Evans and the cluster of women who found their way into his time and occupation.

The limousine had brought him home. Enough with such thought. Time for a glass of wine with Jane. He could only hope she was home too.

Chapter Three:
A Little Domestic Fun

The lock at 24 Sussex was always a bit sticky. After a long day, this nonsense usually frustrated him. He needed rest and balm and, with luck, the comforting words and warmth of Jane. The note on the fridge said she was viewing the Kirov Ballet with her friends Sally and Brian Barrymore. Damn, let's hope some leftovers were in the fridge.

In the comfort of his living room chair he pondered the day. He began to feel quite disturbed by the prospects of alien spying. Were they watching him now? Were they tailing Jane? Was he becoming paranoid?

They had resorted in recent months to a contrived way to make love away from 24 Sussex. Elaine, one of his executive assistants, would book a double room at the Lord Elgin Hotel or the Cartier Place as she saw fit. She would take the keys to the PM's home, and he and Jane would sneak into the booked room while Elaine diverted attention if needed. They no longer trusted the security of their official residence, and Jane shuddered at the prospect of shiny suited spies viewing her private moments.

The RCMP conducted regular sweeps of the house. Devoted guys with modern technology, yet Arthur had limited faith in their effectiveness. In this game, one needed to assume that betrayal always trumped security. And betrayal often came from abroad.

Gerald rang to ask for ten minutes. At 9:30 pm even. Gerald was the chief of the PM's security detail. A good guy. You could even talk soccer with him. He sounded antsy but asked to speak face to face. If he wanted to come here, thought Arthur, he must trust the RCMP sweeping systems.

By the time Gerald arrived, Arthur was refocusing on bigger concerns than his own security. If the Americans had penetrated the firewalls, then perhaps others had too. And the Americans even followed their trails and could then make Canada's public for a favour.

The sight of Gerald, a highly practical prairie type with short hair and military bearing, was a relief. He had proved a reliable companion on both domestic and overseas flights. He never seemed to need baksheesh. The RCMP seemed to have its own currency to facilitate transactions. Better not to ask!

Gerald was sombre. "We have been tailing your wife but have lost her," he revealed as he entered the room.

"What do we do?" Arthur asked quickly. "Can we reach her through the Barrymores?"

Gerald seemed perplexed. "We didn't think she was going to the Barrymores," he replied. "She told us she would be traveling directly to the ballet performance."

"Now I feel terrible," said Arthur. "Has she gone 'walkabout'?"

"We have no electronic tracking on her car, just yours. So she will travel incognito, damn it! Don't you coordinate your lives as married people?" Gerald was at his wit's end, which didn't help Arthur.

Some silence ensued before Arthur managed to stutter, "She'll be back. She's obviously gone somewhere important and couldn't tell me. But neither of us likes to live with uncertainty, so I'm pissed!"

* * *

It was 3 am when Arthur turned over to read the clock. Damn it! She wasn't home yet. The possible outcomes overwhelmed him: kidnapping, assassination, adultery, escape. He called Gerald.

"No word yet," was the first response. "Hang in there," was the second.

He felt he should call their two daughters. Both were in university. It wouldn't be fair to dump all of this on them in the middle of the night. Perhaps Jane had decided to visit Angie in

Kingston. Melanie was out in Victoria recapturing the feel of her father's constituency. These were all idle thoughts.

Somehow he knew that the arrival home of Jane wouldn't happen easily. Another layer of stress had been added to his responsibilities as PM. No counsellor could deal with all of this, even contemplate it. With luck, he would drift off before the alarm at 6 am.

* * *

Shortly after 3:30 am, a bang on the door and its slamming open led to Jane and Gerald. Gerald sounded disgusted.

"Here she is," he blurted out.

"Here I am," she replied petulantly.

"We found her at the Barrymores," Gerald said. "They had kept her presence secret, deliberately to avoid our protectors." Now he started to appear flushed. Oh God, thought Arthur, someone else to placate.

"It is a long story," said Jane. "Let's discuss it in private. Without Gerald"

"OK," Arthur replied, desperate for any mediocre response. And Gerald left the room with mumbled curses and a slammed door.

"I'm sorry," said Jane. "I just couldn't stand another evening shadowed by those big creeps. They are so obviously cops and so obtrusive despite their good intentions."

"OK," Arthur replied. "Spell it out, step by step."

Jane said, "Hang on. I need another glass of Rhone red." She wandered off, kicking shoes wherever and dropping her outer clothes onto available floor space. She didn't seem tired at all. Arthur closed his eyes, expecting another wave of stress outside his control.

When Jane ambled back, she held a glass of wine and had somehow acquired her nightdress and gown. Arthur could only blink and regret his lack of awareness. Late nights and low memories worked together for Arthur.

"I have had it with creeps tailing me to the grocery store, to the theatre, even to the ladies room. This is more than one can ask of any wife. And if I question them, they spout drivel about the country's best interests and their duties to the flag and the people. Really!"

Arthur nodded in understanding. He had contempt for the layers of Ottawa bureaucracy, including the Mounties, who delivered nothing to the public besides salutes and ceremonies. Arthur would occasionally remind everyone from Gerald to Graham, the Clerk, that Canada was a smaller (albeit richer) country, and did not need to strut about contrived world stages. They naturally took immediate umbrage. Arthur wished that he could send them all to Whitehorse on frequent occasions!

Jane continued her rant while Arthur got distracted by her initial complaint. It turned out that Jane had driven off in her car to meet the Barrymores at their home, but then ducked into a parking garage where a pre-booked taxi was waiting. She met the Barrymores at the National Arts Centre and left early by way of their taxi. It seemed too simple. It flummoxed her RCMP tail, though!

Arthur saw the funny side of all of this. Pompous Mounties skewered by smart, cute chick. Jane was more than this, of course. She was an adroit intellectual who could see every side of every question without losing her values.

Jane proffered the central problem with her behaviour: "I duped them, you know," she said. "They will never forgive me."

Arthur acknowledged this with a smile. "Another stack of enemies," he replied. "This must be the job of the PM. Inspiring piles of offended people until the grand electorate joins in." It was time for a new Gilbert and Sullivan jollification. The country needed to see and laugh at the disorganized ritual of Canadian government.

Chapter Four:
Friends or Allies?

Sunday mornings were meant to be different. Arthur tried to make them so. He browsed a stack of favourite newspapers—the front page of the *Globe*, the sports pages of the *London Telegraph*, the editorials and letters in the *Victoria Times-Colonist*. With a bit of luck he got Gordon, his chauffeur, to take him to church for the forty minutes of the Book of Common Prayer communion service (he had long ago persuaded the rector to postpone his homily until the end of the service, after Arthur had sneaked out).

This Sunday would be different, the Prime Minister sensed. The red button on his direct line to the PMO had been blinking for an hour. With moans and groans, he picked it up. After a minute he was speaking with Tasha, a new executive assistant recommended by his constituency office.

"A man named Riggs has called you three times from Washington," she blurted out.

"Does he want to play tennis?" Arthur replied, knowing full well that any Canadian woman under fifty would not have heard of Riggs or Billie Jean King, for that matter. He got a limp "Sorry?" from Tasha, obviously a newcomer. Why else would she be on duty on a cold Sunday morning?

"Tell him I've gone to church, but our Minister of National Defence would be delighted to speak with him. And then call Tom and warn him of what will come."

Arthur wasn't going to let a second-ranked US official get direct access to the first-ranked Canadian one. Get Evans out of bed, he thought, or go play marbles with people your own size.

Arthur figured he needed to skip church again and find his way to his office. He would have a queue of top-priority calls waiting. Right now the only one he really wanted was the one from Tel Aviv.

When he walked into his outer office, he could see Graham acting like a mother hen getting a few PMO staff and some senior PCO people into a cluster of eager "grey" men. Arthur decided to adopt a smooth approach.

"How nice of you all to be here on a Sunday. Thank you, Graham. I suggest you and I have a word and then you can update the others. We have an acute shortage of time today."

In the inner office, Graham seemed placated. Arthur told him the essentials of his earlier discussions with Raj, Tom, Gilles plus David from National Security. Graham already sensed that Arthur's chief of staff should have been included. He knew about the initial breach of the firewalls and how Arthur had intended to contact the White House. The Prime Minister omitted the details of his conversation with the President but mentioned that the Israeli government was eager to help. Nothing seemed to surprise Graham, but he was clearly in turmoil over his secondary role in this affair.

"We will need you to get the public service onside," Arthur volunteered. "But we need to have a special committee meeting after I've spoken with Israel and before the Cabinet meets tomorrow. I'd be really grateful if you could devise a strategy to keep deputies peaceful even if bewildered by their current ignorance."

Edgar, the Israeli PM, could hardly contain himself. "We know how to access WikiLeaks with US-like documents. And we know how to leak the leakers. All we need is the fake information to attribute to the Yanks."

Arthur allowed as how Zimbabwe would be a good target. Few people loved the current president and his followers, but many realised that a scalpel was better than an axe in making changes in Harare. Arthur and Stephen had discussed the possibility of such changes over many months. They now needed to tell the world about how the US was plotting an overthrow. The irony was that the world would applaud. But the Canadians knew that this was simply Phase One. The US would proclaim its innocence throughout sub-Saharan Africa as well as with NATO, Russia and China. Canada's task would be to time Phase Two. It must be soon. The Yanks were no dummies when it came to their security.

Edgar and Arthur laughed aloud. Arthur knew the Israelis had securely scrambled this message across a score of access points. It was almost, but not quite, a secret global initiative.

* * *

Jo Zed had a powerful intellect that he never used. He preferred his instincts, and when his chief of staff told him of a recent communiqué from the Israeli Ambassador, he let out a roar like a lion. The Americans were amassing military resources off the coast of East Africa? Who did he think the peoples of southern Africa were—Grenadians on a Caribbean island? Zulus had a heritage of powerful people treated with disdain, as chronicled by Rhodes and the producers of the movie "Zulu." Who won that battle, the Zulus or the South Wales Borderers led by Michael Caine? A powerful tribe in a now powerful black South Africa, they took a paternal interest in surrounding black nations including Zimbabwe. Besides, South Africans knew that they could barely feed the five million refugees camped near the Zimbabwe border. How many more thousands would flee if the Americans invaded? A coup might be OK, but platoons of parachuted soldiers trained in war-torn Iraq or Afghanistan could be a disaster.

He needed to speak with the Zimbabwean president; he surely must know of this rumour. There were other East African countries directly involved too. What could they know or do? A sub-Saharan strategy might work best.

At that juncture, his secretary alerted him to a call from Tel Aviv. He put off replying. He was smart enough to know that he needed more robust information than a communiqué from Israel. Besides he would rather talk directly with Barry Evans—in Jo's mind, a discussion between equals. He could get his secretary to place a call to Barry who was still in Australia.

* * *

Parliament Hill was a sleepy place on a Sunday, especially in

25

winter months. Today it was teeming with reporters, news cameras and MPs from nearby ridings who could not resist waiting until Monday's publicized announcements.

Gilles felt it best to issue the previous announcements about a Monday morning caucus meeting followed by an afternoon scrum. Louis Blanc, the Party Whip, concurred. They agreed that it was inappropriate to deal sensitive information to only part of the caucus and the House, and it could only stir even more anger out of the permanent "angerphiles" from Northern Alberta. The only downside was the continued effort to sneak people into and outside the East Block with reporters piled up three stories high!

Arthur felt it would be good if Louis called on him first to make a general statement that Canada's security had been compromised and had asked the help of the US, some NATO allies and some Middle Eastern powers to search for the culprits. Until there was some definitive evidence about both who and why, the PM preferred not to alarm either the House (or caucus) about possibilities. He would be prepared to meet again with the caucus (or House) at least once before Thursday when many MPs started to gather their dirty laundry for a journey home.

Rose, his long-time secretary, called again to tell him that Anne Barnaby had an urgent message so he reached Anne by phone, encouraging her to meet with him in her office, which was less likely to be bugged (until tomorrow!). Arthur was glad of the break. A pile of dossiers had needed his signature and those of other ministers whom he found unreliable in their judgements. They held onto their jobs purely for regional representation.

A walk to Anne's new office would be a relief. She greeted Arthur with her big smile and ushered him to the only seat other than her desk chair. She was a short woman who always wore high heels, more for her bearing than her enhanced height.

"I've gone back to my roots," she remarked, using that old joke about changing hair colour. Arthur replied, equally mundanely, that he wished he had enough hair to colour or recolour.

"My NDP friends are really mad about my leaving," she began.

"They even think I'm doing this because you seduced me. But you have never hit on me, ever," she added.

"That's all peculiar and scurrilous," Arthur replied. "You are extremely attractive but I don't have the time or place to seduce you or even love you. I'm married you know."

"That hasn't stopped many men before," was her reply. With that she stood up and, gazing intensely at the PM, lifted her skirt revealing no underwear. "My Germaine Greer fashion look," she whispered.

In what seemed a flash, she sat straddled across Arthur's lap and fished for his zipper. He reached down and clasped her hands. She needed no words to realise his arousal.

"Maybe another time," was all he could nervously stutter. Arthur knew the prospect of an affair could only be self-destructive, and if the Yanks could tap into his email and phone, it could be easy for pimply young cub reporters to find and exploit evidence of his infidelity.

"I do have a job for you, Anne," he remarked, somewhat desperate to change topics. She still straddled him.

"I know from your background as an environmental activist in Vancouver that you were a champion of a big 'local food' movement. I read of your fruit picking in neighbourhood backyards, of constructing maps of drive-by farms in the valley, and of your promotion of community farming plots on allotments in Victoria. We need to put the Feds in a position to help develop these kinds of initiatives in all of our medium-sized and larger cities."

"OK," she said dubiously, shifting her position on Arthur's lap.

"The difference is that I want you to work as a minister of state at Agriculture Canada. That department tends to be invisible outside the farming and food produce people. We need to give it a consumer image and spread that across urban areas, not just in rural Canada."

"It sounds quite interesting," she replied.

Arthur added, "I'll need to alert the Clerk to set up the full mechanisms for a new division in the department and that might take a week or two. So Mum's the word for now."

He managed to push Anne off his lap by standing up. She complied easily.

Wordlessly they looked deeply at each other and, with a brief hug, Arthur turned and left. Anne sat on her desk edge in a very pensive mood. Arthur had changed his plans for her in Cabinet and now she felt piqued by his rejection of her advances. Had she been seduced by his mind but not body?

* * *

Chapter Five:
Confusing and Confused

By the time Barry Evans had found his way back to the sleeping quarters on the plane, Beryl was already dressed and on the phone. She had overheard the conversation between Barry and the Canadian PM, and she needed to mobilize some of her many networks to discover what on earth was happening. Starting with Fred Riggs, Secretary of Defence, she moved through the Department of Defence, CIA, the Canada desk in the State Department, the Ambassador to the UN. The list was about to explode. This was Beryl's world—working and developing networks to learn from and build big coalitions of diverse interests.

Beryl knew that she couldn't actually raise the myriad chiefs from their slumbers. But a phone call to their "en garde" assistants could stimulate an early reply as soon as they became cognizant of life; that is, awake.

Beryl thrived on networks. You never survived in New Jersey politics without a series of networks. Loyalty in that culture was intense especially in her district in Newark. But loyalty was tradable too for most partisans, Republican and Democrat. Beryl, with an absurd English first name due to her war bride mother, was in fact a Rossini which placed her in the throes of Italian culture. Well-mannered second generation immigrants like Beryl could enjoy respectability and deal with power on the streets, in the clubs, in the churches. Activity in multiple networks gave her tradable information and reserves of loyal compatriots. She had worked this advantage into a congressional seat, then a governorship.

Beryl had had aspirations for the White House. She knew over time that her personality, her natural charm, her understanding of policy issues did not resonate with most Democratic Party bosses outside the East. Even her accent seemed to put others on edge. She never had the money or interest to get educated downstate at Princeton. That would have been a phoney veneer. She was street smart, energetic and able to deal with the informed elites who ran New Jersey largely for themselves.

Barry's arrival elicited immediate questions from Beryl.

"Who the hell is this turd, Arthur Jones? What kind of game is he playing, calling us this way?"

Beryl's instincts took her immediately to ideas of conspiracy, of revenge, of manipulation.

Barry yawned a reply. "Canadian prime ministers, including Jones, are constitutionally boring and obliging. A spade is never called a spade. It could come out sounding like an implement that might be construed as a technical instrument for moving stuff from one place to another."

He roared with laughter at his own joke. It earned a smile from Beryl, but she remained suspicious. Tomorrow's "to do" list would include getting her assistants to start investigating. She'd leave it to them to see if they could summon the patience to collaborate with the earnest public servants in the State Department.

* * *

Canberra was in its usual immaculate state. Litter collected, cigarette butts swept away, streetscapes orderly. Hot too in the summer. "They clean up good," as the Yanks would say.

Barry made his twenty-minute remarks to a joint Senate–House assembly, all about friendship, cooperation, reliability, common values and concerns. The Aussies loved it. Status, rather than equality, with world powers was their concern. It was the need to be treated as a good mate, one of the team, and never as colonial boys.

Beryl had a chance to exchange brief comments with the Foreign Secretary. Their agenda for tomorrow's meeting had been fixed some weeks previously. She remarked how much she shared Australian concerns about illegal immigrants, the challenges of a wealthy, powerful China, the opportunities of developing a full western culture even in the southern hemisphere. She actually wanted to know what they thought of Arthur Jones, the Canadian Prime Minister. She never really understood why networks like the Commonwealth could ever generate an emotional tinge. The Aussies might know Jones through this linkage.

The state dinner was more of the same—lots of diplomatic protocol and flattering commentaries on two nation states. In 24 hours they would be returning to the US. The main business tomorrow would be to announce officially the creation of a new South Pacific alliance enveloping not just Micronesia, but also the semi-circle of island territories east of Singapore. Both Barry and Beryl hoped they could get some private time with their counterparts from Australia. They had requested such from their organizers, who felt that uncontrolled time on any agenda could lead to bad consequences. Meanwhile Beryl had to hope that, back home, some information was gathering for her return. Barry, as usual, felt that it was another "bloody tempest in teapot."

* * *

In Arthur's office, Stephen was tracking these southern hemisphere developments. He sensed how protective the US presidency could be to charges of maligning and mischief with the politics of allies. But he knew their track record was poor. He sympathised with Castro in Cuba, Jagan in Trinidad and Chavez in Venezuela. And he also understood how, since the Iraq debacle, US foreign policy was now circumspect.

Stephen kept in touch with Arthur with a twice-daily call in addition to ad hoc communications. Arthur was hard to find many days. He was trying to fashion the kind of speech and agenda that would rally his caucus and Parliament to his side. He knew they wouldn't have the stomach for revenge. He knew, however, that they all expected a hypothetical victory.

* * *

When Barry and Beryl returned to their (separate) sleeping quarters in Government House, the messages were piled high on their desks by their assistants who were smart enough to avoid a ruckus in the midst of a state dinner. Barry had received phone calls from the President of Zimbabwe, the President of South Africa, the

UN Secretary General, the Prime Minister of Britain, the list went on. Unfortunately, there were too many to reply to all at one go. He would need to have staff signal to them that he could be making a public statement tomorrow morning before the announcement of a new alliance at the Parliament buildings.

Beryl too had communiqués from fellow foreign ministers in NATO and Southern Africa. She could rely on Barry's public statement as a tactful response.

Neither of them could understand how a rumour about a US invasion of Zimbabwe could gain credence. Most world powers knew that the nearest US forces were deployed in Korea and their nearest aircraft carriers were in the North Pacific and the Mediterranean. This seemed to be an instant worldwide rumour. Beryl refused to believe all of this was an accident. Barry felt that an unspecified Eastern power was intent on undermining his credibility and that of close allies like Canada.

* * *

The morning took them back to the Prime Minister's offices in the Parliament buildings. The meeting was originally scheduled to begin at 10:00 am, Canberra time, but Barry's staff had asked for an earlier appointment at 9:00 am.

"Let me say right away, Mr. President," the Prime Minister said even before they had finished shaking hands, "how proud we are of you, your country and your leadership on this horrible issue of Zimbabwe." Barry was stunned.

"We have lobbied the UK, the Commonwealth and the Republic of South Africa to marshal some forces to get Zimbabwe back onto a peaceful democratic track—and as the breadbasket of Southern Africa."

Barry let him finish. The Prime Minister went on, "We will pledge up to 2,000 troops in a combat and supporting role, starting as soon as the transport logistics permit. We thank you so much."

"This is all lies and rumours," Barry responded in an atypical, abrasive manner. "The United States has never contemplated invasions in Southern Africa and we've always respected the positions of the countries there, that they can resolve their own problems. We thought and still think that the Zimbabwe situation will evolve and a democratic regime will be the outcome."

Now the Aussie Prime Minister looked stunned. "This has embarrassed not only you but me too," he shouted in reply. "Goddamn it! You had best cancel our lunchtime conference and press statement. You'll be needed in Washington and we'll need to work out some alternative times for celebrating the new alliance— perhaps midway like Honolulu."

Barry murmured ready agreement. He needed to review the speech he would give in a short while. He asked if the PM would stand with him for this statement.

"Of course," was the quick reply

The two met briefly before they emerged for their statements. The press looked shocked, then amused and then anxious. Arthur watched all of this on TV.

"Yes!" he declared, jumping out of his desk chair.

* * *

Chapter Six:
Some Past and Some Present

Arthur never thought of himself as devious. He preferred the word "strategic" because it acknowledged select behaviours that did not challenge his ethical norms and rules. He did allow that some societal rules were crazy or even out of date. But most were functional guides around which he could manoeuvre.

It took him many years to develop such self-reflection. Brought up as an only child in what was then a small, affordable house in Fairfield, Arthur's mother fashioned a large set of norms and rules that she vigorously enforced with emotional bribes and threats. He might have benefited more if his Dad had lived—some kind of counterbalance to maternal micromanagement. Perhaps they might have collaborated and driven him totally neurotic. He knew that much of his childhood, especially as a teen, was weary and unnecessarily complicated.

He walked to Vic High daily, meeting friends en route. They were all keen "dramatic artists" and worked at plays in school and in the local church. They all seemed to feel a surge of emotional release when portraying characters other than their own. Occasionally they developed comedy sketches, with lots of mimicry and occasional rude jokes. Their school teachers were obvious targets for fun both on stage and in school rooms. He grew up with his friends as a second family. And he survived what seemed to him to be a turbulent youth by getting excellent grades almost as a method of disguising the real Arthur.

Arthur fell in love with the drama of politics. He and his friends were first exposed to real world politics by attending a small meeting in the Empress Hotel that featured former PM John Diefenbaker as the main speaker. Those were the days of symbolic national politics with inflamed debates about flags, stamps, bilingualism, even names for airlines and government agencies. Arthur loved it! He could see all sides of these debates and was challenged to become the underdog no matter the cause.

His friend Alex was asked to help out in the forthcoming provincial election, and Arthur was keen to go along. He quickly discovered that this was his "mission." Elections were wonderful. They were all about competition—between parties on doorsteps, in poll districts, in constituencies (and Victoria had three seats in its provincial constituency) and then in province or country. All of these competitions happened virtually simultaneously. All required different strategies, and many were limited only by informal rules devised by gentlemen! For Arthur, the only real constraints were time and energy. The New Democratic Party (NDP) was full of young Arthurs, keen and convinced. He knew politics was his vocation.

In those days, the NDP never won a seat in Victoria at either level of government. But it formed the official opposition provincially, if not nationally. Arthur was soon off to Vancouver for party meetings and more party meetings. Policy was largely developed in face-to-face meetings and confirmed by typed letters. It required the seemingly endless energy of young Arthurs, both male and female.

The female "Arthurs" were in a decided minority. Arthur discovered, however, that there were women his age who actually liked politics, its passion and its drama. The ones in the NDP did not offer a conflict between entertainment and politics. They knew politics trumped all, except perhaps late-night sex in the Travelodge (as it became called) on Granville Street.

Arthur lived at home and went to the spanking new University of Victoria, 2000 students in total in the redbrick enlarged normal school on Lansdowne Road. It was a much longer walk from home, and bikes were considered quite a bourgeois hobby. So he begged lifts and got taxis and complained about the lack of buses.

At the end of his undergraduate studies, Arthur was awarded a Governor General's medal for outstanding grades and, with a scholarship and some summer earnings in a lumber yard, could just about afford law school at the University of British Columbia (UBC).

Mark Sproule-Jones

He supplemented his income by delivering Christmas mail and taking a job on Saturday nights waiting tables at the White Spot on Granville, as well as accepting some marking assistance work at the school. These of course were frustrating as he saw his ambition curbed by lack of money. He could, in contrast, repeat the names and grades of at least 25% of his law school year. He wondered if a C in undergraduate studies was all that UBC really required if you had connections. Damned upper class again, controlling the educational opportunities of working class kids.

Arthur wanted to prepare for his bar exams with an Ottawa law firm and then use his articling prestige to establish a political base on Vancouver Island. His ambition was rarely frustrated. His social skills were now quite well attuned to persons, contexts and places.

It was Jane who gave all of these events some meaning. She went to U Vic too, a couple of years after him. She came from a large family in Fairfield, but it wasn't until Grade 12 that he noticed her. They were in a small advanced history class for gifted students. She wouldn't let him pronounce with glib statements. She could challenge him to prove his points and develop his conclusions. Not even his teachers were that astute. They became quite good friends in a school environment.

At U Vic they lost touch until their junior years when they both took American Government from an outrageous professor who seemed to grade from rote and ignore all but compliant women. By this time, Arthur was constantly outraged by most things, from professors to the H-bomb to his mother's relative penury. Jane seemed to provide a seasoning of calm for his behaviour. She employed similar skills in resisting his fumbling efforts at seduction.

It wasn't until Arthur was in law school and Jane had gone to Queen's for an MA that they realised how much they missed each other. Regular letters were necessary plus an expensive Friday phone call. Their first Christmas back in Victoria unlocked their passions and they both knew that their bodies were designed for each other. Even a touch, perhaps a glance, brought a blush to Jane's cheeks. It was not going to be easy to contain their lust in these few years before the pill became fully established.

So when Arthur eventually got into a Victoria law firm, Jane returned to Victoria with her MA in hand and few job prospects. Arthur hated the frustrations in their lives—money and an unequal distribution of such, privilege and its favours, family connections and their own limited networks. It seemed made, in Arthur's eyes, for a crusade against established interests.

* * *

Arthur often thought of those student days when in Parliament in Ottawa. They brought a smile to his face as he recollected how his youthful zeal convinced him that every rule and norm could disappear with rhetoric, comradeship and hard work. Now in these years, he really needed strategy, even devious strategy. The competition was still there. The cunning of competitors always seemed present and a threat. You never knew who would be carrying the knife.

It seemed that the best plan was to set the agenda and keep competitors and favourites off guard. Laurels were never to rest on. Phase Two of his counter-spying initiatives needed developing and implementing.

* * *

Arthur knew he had twelve hours, at best, before the Americans figured out Phase One. And they were pretty good at retaliation especially with various military bases around the borders. Further confusion was not just possible but essential at this juncture.

He scurried to work early, calling Stephen en route. Like Arthur, Stephen was a morning person, even in those Ottawa mornings when the icicles hung off the eavestroughs and sidings and sensible people rolled under a second duvet. They also both distrusted cell phone security, but knew they could fix up innocuous matters like dates at the office. He asked Stephen to get hold of the original subcommittee and ask them to show up no later than 8 am. Arthur wanted Gilles to be there especially. He had a Jesuitical bent, ideal for these circumstances.

He telephoned Jane on his way to the office and woke her up. "Just checking in," he said. "Masses of 'to do' things required an early start," he added.

37

He sorely missed her counsel at this stage. She could figure out American counterstrategies better than his official advisors. "Come by for a coffee if you can," he added surprisingly. She sensed this was code for soon if possible.

Arthur slammed the door to his office almost in Stephen's face. They knew each other well enough to avoid any hints of umbrage. Stephen had been a tall, lanky intern from Hamilton when he came to Arthur's attention. Arthur's translation from provincial politics had not been tidy. He needed willing and energetic bodies who could implement instructions and ask for more. Arthur immediately knew that Stephen was his kind of man even though he had barely passed his second decade.

"Let's talk in your car," Arthur blurted out before either of them could discard their overcoats. "We can drive around relatively undetected for a while and then we can walk through the mall for ten minutes. This is critical watch time." Stephen nodded in agreement. His '06 Corolla attracted little attention at the best of times.

Arthur took the risk of talking in the car about Phase Two. "Did we quarantine the items on the hard drives that were invaded by the US?" he asked.

"Yes," replied Stephen who knew a week ago that this kind of reaction defence would be needed at any time.

"That's good," said Arthur, trying not to sound like Richard Burton in "The Spy Who Came in From the Cold"! They both tried not to giggle.

After parking, Arthur began to suggest a strategy for Phase Two, emphasizing all the time that this was a draft, a suggestion, a set of items for further thought when they returned to the office. He also mentioned a deadline of noon to get the basics in place. Much now depended on Arthur's meeting with Tom, scheduled in briefly before 8 am and to be resumed after the others had left.

When Tom arrived he was unshaven and looked haggard. Not even his misspent youth in Montreal could anticipate his overwork and anxiety in the last few days.

"We can do it, we think," he said immediately. "We have been able to trace back the routes into our defence server from your virus, and then from your virus into a series of pathways at least to the stage where we know we are in DC offices. It could take us a day to penetrate the exact source in the Pentagon."

Arthur grimaced. "We may have to release our own virus and hope it won't be detected as it tries the millions of combinations of possible entry points into the full depths of Washington."

"I agree," said Tom. "We can work at time zero and hope for delay as the Americans follow up our strategy. They will catch us for sure, but we may outrun them enough to shut down their servers around the world."

Arthur and Tom had speculated on this possibility for some months but mostly in anticipation of it being sourced by an unfriendly power. Now it was being done by good old compliant Canada. The Americans will not be able to reveal how their system was penetrated without acknowledging that the access routes were of their own construction. They had started this.

The subcommittee meeting started late almost inevitably. Arthur outlined his strategy, and Tom interjected on the occasional technical matter. John expressed the feelings they all had, one of deep anxiety if the trick did not work and reprisals came over the border.

Arthur anticipated these comments. "We are very much a client state of America," he allowed. "But we must have some kind of line to distinguish our business from theirs. They would not do this to any other friendly country. They have come to see us as patsies who won't make a fuss!"

Tom got up to leave. Arthur hoped that the overnight sweeping of the room had been thorough and their discussion was not overheard.

"Mum's the word and fingers crossed," he announced as people started to leave. "We'll have a secret way of retaliating that the Americans cannot announce or condemn. If there are any future reprisals, the episode will make a fabulous movie."

They shook hands and hugged before leaving. Arthur found himself alone in the room. He loved Shakespeare, including the "exit followed by a bear" comment in. He always wanted to play that bear.

Chapter Seven:
Some Fun and Games

Arthur ambled back to his office, avoiding the kind of eye contact that might have invited a conversation. Times were tense. Issues could wait. He wondered about Jane, her whereabouts, her advice. He avoided thinking about rebellious rumours in his Cabinet and caucus. There were always some dedicated and well-practised "shit disturbers" no matter what he did or said.

His outer office was packed. Stephen, God bless him, had anticipated his needs. All thirty or so of his assistants had been summoned to hear the latest and confirm their team morale. The large majority of his office spent their time answering the mail, over 200 at the last count. Then there were the bunch that Stephen thought necessary to monitor (or rather spy on) department recommendations. The closest group were the advance travel unit, the media group now swelled with two young persons monitoring social networks, the protocol unit, and then a free forming group assigned and reassigned to the moving "peril problems" that always landed in the PM's office. Thank God for Stephen. Never flustered, always happy with reorganization.

When he shut the door behind him, the assembly clapped. He was so impressed but also nonplussed. Stephen must have clued them into the torments of Phases One and Two, but even he did not know the full story. Arthur felt it essential to bring his loyal team into focus.

"Thank you, thank you," he began. The silence was deafening.

"I should tell you that our plans are OK so far. I expect Stephen sketched Phase One for you in the broadest terms, without implicating any particular county in the attack on our sovereignty.

Phase Two, a bit of retaliation to assert that we are no compliant state has now been implemented. We have sent a virus down the pathways that enabled the antagonists to penetrate our system. We expect our response to reach its destination—the source of this problem—by roughly noon. We think and hope and even pray a bit that the protagonist will not declare that it used its power to attempt to decimate a friendly ally just for the hell of it.

"I take that back," Arthur continued. "We don't know why this has happened, but we are determined to avoid the label of 'patsy' or 'butterfingers' from an aggressive ally with not enough to do."

It took a minute before anyone responded. Someone with scruffy hair, who must be new to the team, asked out loud, "So do we know the enemy?"

Arthur immediately reacted. "No enemies for us. Just stupid aggressors."

"Sorry," he added. "We need the right kind of spin on this. We are responding to an important invasion in a way to tell the world we are not a client state nor do we want to be."

Arthur felt the rhetoric was a bit too much for this sophisticated crowd. So he added, "We are going one step at a time. Now that Phase Two has begun, we think the protagonist (your enemy) will be too embarrassed to respond and admit that they lack loyalty to one of their closest allies."

Before another question, Arthur posed one for the assembly. "We have three to four hours before Question Time, and we will surely be asked to clarify all of the rumours. I'd ask you to organize yourselves into small groups and let Stephen distill what you have found out in your dealings across the Hill. What will I be asked? From whom? With what tone? With any approvals?"

This is exactly what the team wanted. It was participation, a call for loyalty, a need to bond together for their boss, for Parliament, and (for some) for their own country's survival.

Arthur went into his inner office and flopped onto his chair with relief. He had learned to love his team. Energetic, reliable, imaginative, dedicated and organized in a rational way by Stephen.

While he found Ottawa to be a fragmented, dramatic system of independent actors, he had constructed a unit of devoted support for times good and bad.

* * *

Arthur remembered that he needed to keep Edgar, the Israeli PM, fully informed of events. That proved to be an energizing call, and Edgar offered to sponsor a worldwide conference on the topic of "e-spying" and invite various keynote speakers including Barry Evans. That guy was irrepressible; no wonder the Palestinians found him to be a "handful."

On hanging up, Arthur felt a little disconsolate. So far, events had proceeded according to Plan A. In his thirty years of politics, nothing seemed ever to proceed according to Plan A. He was always a trimmer, moving positions and plans a little this way or that to accommodate objectives. He never lost sight of the goals intended, unlike most of his peers. His ability to see and operationalize from general principles was what brought him the respect and approval of the public at large.

He phoned Jane again. He needed her world views and temperament too. No damn answer, either at home or on her cell phone. He buzzed his secretary to ask if Jane had left a message. Nothing. This was very odd and Arthur felt even very maddened. It was so out of character for both of them to be apart intellectually and emotionally in the middle of a political crisis.

So he called Anne. There wasn't really a legitimate "so" in his thinking. He needed consolation at least and a long rant at most. He was in a risk-taking mood, which had proved dangerous and self-destructive for him on previous occasions.

Anne answered at the first ring. "You are lucky you called just now," she said. "I have a family crisis at home and am planning to get out of this town on the 4 pm."

Arthur realised at once how little he knew about her. "I'm sorry," he replied.

"You wouldn't know," she said. "I leave my two teenagers with my mother while I am here. Their Dad is hopeless. He forgets the simplest things and is unreliable all the time. I left him ten years ago because of unreliability. He cannot operate a family unless the little woman stays at home and organizes everyone's life."

"I recognize the problem," Arthur replied. "Perhaps you should go now, have a bite to eat at the airport—a late lunch perhaps—and then a quiet couple of hours to catch up on correspondence while waiting for your plane."

"No," was Anne's reply. "I have some time. I could get the 7 pm plane out of Toronto if needed. Why are you calling?"

Challenged like this, Arthur felt quite embarrassed, like a small boy caught masturbating by a parent.

"I need to see you, to relate to you, to love you," he blurted out. He wasn't even sure he believed these words. "I've regretted our previous encounter. I got scared and damn respectable."

Anne's tone of voice changed. The business woman became the affectionate and lustful friend for whom Arthur yearned. "We can make up for past mistakes," she whispered.

"I'll come over," said Arthur. "Your place?"

"Come to my office first," she replied. "We can then go in my car and skip the media throng."

"OK." Arthur responded. "I'll get my driver to take my dummy person—an EA from my office wearing a flat hat and a duffle coat—across the river to meet with Stephen there. It should take half an hour at best."

They both felt the anticipation. Lust and loving to come. And they were both determined to make this work. Arthur felt that somehow this was Jane's doing and more...........

* * *

An hour later, when Arthur finally got to Anne's office, she was close to frantic with worry, anger, regret. He apologised of course. He recognized that apologies were never sufficient even if necessary.

"The details served up everything," he said. "Fortunately Stephen was part of the plan and he is Mr. Fix-It for me. Besides I'm here."

Within a minute, Anne was on the carpeted floor with nothing on below her waist. Arthur joined her with a comparable lack of attire. They pleased each other for a few minutes and whispered the kinds of words that only lovers could express.

"Open up," said Arthur, and soon the immaculate congress was in progress, capturing a full panoply of emotions. It ended sooner than both wished of course. But it was a moment of content, of completion. And it was a moment to savour in recollections to come.

* * *

Arthur's office was still packed with assistants who scurried around answering telephone calls, Facebook posts and voice mails all under Stephen's surveillance. He held the fort so well.

Arthur asked for the "most important list" of people he must call. He could squeeze one or two in before Question Period, he hoped. First, however, he tried Gerald to ask if he had knowledge of Jane's whereabouts.

"No, Prime Minister," was the immediate reply. "After the last incident, we try to keep a very discreet distance. There was a report from a regular posting at the airport that she was seen checking into a WestJet flight to Victoria, so possibly she could be there or in Toronto, Winnipeg or Calgary where the plane stops."

"Thanks Gerald. I'll try my daughter in Victoria, as well as my constituency office there. Perhaps they might know something," he added.

That left him only three minutes or so before he walked to the Commons. Graham needed an immediate approval of committee meetings for the next four weeks. Mundane but important, so he initialled the email and got an EA to walk it over to the Privy Council Office.

The Commons was in its usual uproar. Questions had begun, and Arthur had already been accused of avoiding Parliament and subverting democracy. Fortunately the Government benches erupted with applause and a standing ovation upon his entry. Good old Gilles and good old Luc.

When the noise subsided a little, he addressed the Speaker and asked for approval to make a short statement and then take questions from the other party leaders. Everyone consented, even the Speaker.

"Mr. Speaker, as many members of this House know, our communications system was penetrated late last week by an unknown source. We quarantined our files, probably too late for full security. We then attempted to discover the source of the attack, using our own security systems in the departments of Border Security and National Defence. The US President kindly agreed to have the CIA help in the tracking. We are still unsure who is the computer thief or for what organization he or she works. Given the crisis in the US over the international rumour of a planned invasion of Zimbabwe, we cannot rely on too much help from Washington at this time. We have pledges of help from many NATO countries and others with whom we enjoy cordial diplomatic relations.

"I'd be happy, Mr. Speaker, to elaborate on my comments by answering questions from the floor."

Mr. Katich, the Opposition Leader, rose to his feet to ask the first question. Arthur always thought he looked like a scruffy emu wandering the Australian outback, hair askew, small head on a long neck, and a body that was ill fitted for any chair. While these thoughts always made Arthur smile, they did not help his concentration on the question at hand.

Katich asked why the Commons had not been recalled for a special session as soon as the computer systems infiltration was known, and why only government MPs seemed to have full knowledge of the events. "Does the Prime Minister not understand that Parliament, not the executive branch, is the centre of our democracy?"

Arthur responded without a trace of hostility. "Events unfolded too quickly for us to reorganize parliamentary dates. MPs were already in their home constituencies or packing to get there. Does not the Opposition Leader recognize the size of this country? It takes six or so hours to fly to Victoria, while he can get a commuter plane to take him to his waterside condo in Toronto Harbour in little more than an hour."

"Supplementary, Mr. Speaker."

Katich never gave up. "If our defence records and strategies are known by another power, what has the Prime Minister done to alert the civil authorities about possible terrorist attacks? Has the RCMP been brought into the picture yet?"

"I share the concerns of the Leader of the Opposition," Arthur began. "We needed to focus first on our intelligence units, then on the government apparatus, and all the while talk to people from allied countries. No one is excluding the RCMP, and we expect and understand that they will discuss these issues informally with CSIS and others, before we advance an official order to them. Time has been very short, Mr. Speaker, but we are enlisting the full and complete aid of public authorities right across Canada."

Arthur realized that much of his answer was an exaggeration but the hypothetical course of events could happen anyway in the next few days.

Bert Condon was next in line, as leader of the third party. Always abrasive, a lover of verbal fights, an "old school" socialist who knew all the words to "The Red Flag" song, he had been appointed to rescue the party from oblivion. No one doubted his sincerity. But everyone doubted the veracity of his statements. The question he asked was typical Bert:

"When is the Prime Minister going to get off his rear end and find out who were the invaders and why wasn't there an advanced warning for the country?"

"Mr. Speaker," Arthur replied with a grin, "our government is never on its rear end, and neither am I. The intelligence communities of the world rely on secrecy and spying, and only after the fact are the details known. Besides, Canada is no superpower. We made a mistake. We did not think our secrets would interest any other world powers."

That brought forth the cries of "shame," "traitor," "disgusting" from the opposition benches.

Arthur added, "I look forward to meeting with the leaders of all 4 parties to give them a candid, confidential opinion of what has transpired and what will, we hope, happen. This House can work together for the sake of country."

Maurice, the leader of the fourth party, insisted on speaking in French and, while Arthur had some capacity, he preferred to use the audio equipment to get the full story. He pushed in the earphones to hear the translator tell him and others that the leader of the fourth party wanted to assure the House that separatists would never resort to undermining the government's information system. The Speaker had to insist that he ask a question and avoid such apologetics.

"Can the PM assure us that our communications invasion was not in any way linked to the US crisis over Zimbabwe?"

"Ah ha," thought Arthur. So there is a mole in my office who harbours some interest in Quebec separation. He made a mental note to have this checked out.

"We understand that many advanced countries were made aware of the Zimbabwe hoax. We certainly were, probably about 24 hours or so after our loss of full security. We find it difficult to link Canada with Zimbabwe although we have pressed the Zimbabweans to conduct free and fair elections and enforce full human rights in their country."

Maurice had a supplementary as well. "Did the PM offer Canada's help to the US to discover the source of the hoax?"

Arthur allowed as to how he has been in constant touch with American diplomats in Ottawa and in Washington, and that he prefers to deal with such issues in confidence and only when the help extended could be effective. Arthur loved to speed up his replies to questions from Maurice. Maurice was too vain to use the translation service and yet not good enough to understand the rapid use of long English words.

Arthur then addressed the Speaker. "Mr. Speaker, our Foreign Affairs Minister as well as our House Leader are happy to answer any further questions on this issue. I will be keeping the House informed in different ways. You must excuse me now, as I need to return telephone calls from a number of world leaders. Thank you."

With that, Arthur left the chamber, shaking hands with a number of supporters on the way out. He was increasingly concerned about Jane. And the incident with Anne was pricking his conscience.

* * *

Chapter Eight:
Jane at Large

Arthur often paced the floors of his houses in Ottawa or in Victoria. It was probably due to anxiety or stress of some kind.

"Damn it, Jane. Why pick this time to disappear?" He now had people looking for her in BC, Toronto, Ottawa and even in London. The Mounties had been given carte blanche authority to search.

Meanwhile Arthur wondered about tomorrow's questions in the House. He needed something new to say. Ironically it was the Americans who solved this quandary. The fax in his study at home was now clanking out a sheet of typed paper, forwarded no doubt by another standby executive assistant. The fax read:

"The United States of America wishes to announce to governments and to peoples around the world that our defence system has been severely compromised. Hopefully it will soon be restored.

"Some power or persons has sent a virus into the computers at the Pentagon and we found it impossible to isolate it before the entire military computer system had shut down.

"We think that the responsible parties were the same anarchists who perpetrated the worldwide hoax last week to the effect that the United States was preparing to invade Zimbabwe. We suspect this is a different group of terrorists, neither the 9/11 crowd nor the WikiLeaks people. All clues are being followed to help us identify the source and bring these people to justice.

"Meanwhile we have asked some of our allies to loan us part of their best computer systems so that our air force, navy and land forces may remain operational. Great Britain is our ally for NATO countries, Japan for the Far East, Israel for the Mid East, Australia for the South Pacific, and Mexico for mid and South America. We hope that we can restore our own operations within the week, and our experts are working with Google to reconstruct an information holding system for our new operations.

"Some emergency operations are in place. No civil aircraft will be allowed to take off from, fly over or land in America at least until Thursday noon next week. Everyone crossing our borders or entering our ports will need an entry visa and proof of their recent itinerary over the past week. Without these documents, all visitors will have to postpone travel plans to the US until next Thursday noon.

"Full radio and telephone communications with our overseas military will be facilitated by our embassies and offices around the world.

"We thank you in advance for your patience. Rest assured we will find the source of these problems. Meanwhile I call on all of you to pray for the United States in these hours of critical need."

Arthur was quite impressed with the speed with which Evans and his staff plus agency people in DC had constructed this novel and civil defence machinery. They had obviously studied and learned from the 9/11 incidents, and had quickly enlisted the aid of foreign allies. Fortunately the thousands of domestic police officers and private security forces could ensure the usual levels of law and order at home. Normalcy was an American word but very useful in these kinds of circumstances.

Arthur could find out more by telephone tonight, from Raj as well as Stephen, and then fashion a framework for government policy tomorrow. Now he had only Jane's absence to worry about until dawn. He hoped for some sleep. He never operated well on less than seven hours a night...

* * *

Jane always felt that she was a reasonable soul, indeed that she had a reasonable soul. She enjoyed her virtues of empathy and logic, as did Arthur. She made a perfect partner for an ambitious politician. Her only regret was that it became too difficult to sustain

51

a teaching career with disabled students and fulfill the role of chief policy and political advisor to the PM. In politics, no one day ever seems like the last or the next. Or, as Harold Wilson claimed, politics changed by the hour.

Jane was also strikingly beautiful, tall and blonde. She did not mind using her charm to promote her causes. Arthur always felt secure whenever Jane took over a file.

Jane thought that the Zimbabwe hoax had been great fun and that it served the Americans right. But her reasonable soul told her that the virus attack was "over the top." It was all well and good to practice non-harmful practical jokes and puncture the pomposity of man, woman and even country. It was a different thing, she felt, to invade the military defences of the strongest world power. Canada was largely defenceless, and Arthur's retaliation needed re-thinking.

Because it was too late to retract the virus, Arthur's strategy needed buffering by supplementary plans to place the blame elsewhere or at least to put it into a wider plausible context. So Jane decided to consult a former BC Premier and friend of the family who lived largely alone on Cortes Island, between Campbell River (on Vancouver Island) and Powell River (on the BC mainland). He wasn't really alone as he had a beautiful golden retriever, Stella, and could take his "putt-putt" boat around the spur and get to the island village.

Jane knew that Dave could keep a secret and had a lifetime of connections to the Canadian and American military. He had been an army "brat" before settling into undergraduate history and law at the University of British Columbia. Jane had the idea of getting Dave to sound out his contacts in the US first and then help her to construct a different tale of the virus attack.

She needed complete anonymity to do this. Not even Arthur should know. She caught a red-eye special to Victoria and then rented a car to drive up-island where the Campbell River ferry would take her to Cortes. Her navy blue duffle coat and hat would attract little attention, and she used her maiden name to book the flight and car rental. She had developed supplementary identification cards (as had Arthur) in order to make anonymous holiday get-aways All of this was done outside the scrutiny of Gerald, the Mounties, and the PMO staff.

"Shit." Dave uttered his usual expletive while he cooked a late breakfast for them both. Arthur sometimes let a good idea drive out better ones, and Dave and Jane knew how heady it could feel for Arthur to pursue the virus retaliation. The reasonable side of Jane's personality needed to be exercised, and Arthur's schedule left little time in the hours before Jane went west.

"Let us spell out options," Jane began.

"And identify our closest friends," added Dave. "Our links with Israel make them complicit allies. Let us make a list."

* * *

"I should find a way to tell Arthur that I'm safe and healthy," Jane muttered as they made the list. "He deserves no less and, on past form, he will be stressed, angry and anxious."

Dave did not reply. No advice was sometimes better than any advice.

"Perhaps I should ask my daughter to tell the constituency office in Victoria that I'm OK." Dave still said nothing.

"Will that be sufficient to conceal my tracks?" Jane asked directly.

Dave did not hesitate much in replying, "Probably not. You have a major dilemma. I'd put out a message to both of your daughters for both of them to say they had seen you and you were OK, just AWOL for now. If you can think of a third person, go ahead. Single tracks are never conducive to security."

Dave agreed that they would use his cell phone from the village pier to call both daughters and, if they were not there, Dave rather than Jane would leave a terse, ambiguous message. Jane felt a little better.

Dave thought it best for Jane to stay overnight and perhaps the next day at the "Institute for Self-Actualization" located on Cortes. It was full of people in retreat, in escape and in confusion, and Jane was like many a regular guest, a post-menopausal blonde Canadian with grown children.

Jane shuddered a little. She preferred her left-brain thinking to group love-in efforts to help people cope. She would go, of course. Dave would get her there after the phone call and pick her up the following morning to brief her on the news, as he knew it. It wasn't the best arrangement, though Jane actually thought that a one-day retreat might bring her some solace. She needed the practice of self-reflection.

* * *

Word of Jane's absence had leaked already, less than 24 hours before she arrived at the Institute on Cortes. Jane felt it was at least a plausible place to go. The press would not understand but she knew her friends would, and she hoped that Arthur would eventually understand. She spent the evening talking quietly with some of the guests. They were too polite or perhaps ignorant to let on that they knew she was the PM's wife. Of course, Jane knew that if they watched TV that night she would be recognizable.

Arthur was close to frantic one moment and depressed the next. It made his job much more difficult; even the routine duties seemed too onerous. He spent some time making telephone calls to top politicians in a number of countries. Edgar proved a grand partner, full of optimism and humour. Barry Evans did not return an initial call from Arthur. The House was humourless, and Question Period posed the perennial problem of "how do you say you know nothing" in twenty different ways. Arthur began to feel more and more beleaguered and more and more lonely without Jane.

Carol was Arthur's chief media person, and she provided some advice on keeping the press and TV away from questions about Jane. The media knew that the computer hacking incident was still under investigation, and so they decided to investigate Jane's absence themselves because the PMO seemed to know nothing.

Arthur anticipated the weekend ahead and got Rose to book a first-class ticket to Victoria to get him away for a while. He could spend a busy Saturday doing constituency work, something he always enjoyed. He felt his vocation return as he helped real people solve problems with bureaucracy and other sources of complications of social life.

In the late afternoon of the Tuesday in question, 48 hours after Jane had "disappeared," Arthur's raucous plans were changed by a call from Melanie, his daughter in Victoria. It was on a land line and probably monitored by the RCMP, among others.

"Dad, I've received a message from Mum via Vera at the constituency office and from Dave Bond on Cortes saying that she is OK and for you not to worry. She is trying to discover the solution to difficulties you both have had in the last few weeks. Dad, what does this mean? Are you separating? Why is she there and not at home either in Victoria or Ottawa?"

Arthur could hear the sobs. "She has kept me in the dark, I'm afraid. I've been so busy with some crises here at work that we haven't had a chance to discuss these events or even spend time together. This is the first news I've had of where she might be. Thank God for that. Can you find out more? Ask Vera where Dave was calling from and see if you can retrace the calls. She can't be far away. I think we all, as a family, need to talk through the issues."

Arthur added, "I should tell you that my phone is tapped by the RCMP and perhaps others so I'd throw your cell away right now and buy a new one. I'll pay. We want to keep family matters out of politics if we can."

"I love you, Dad," Melanie replied. "Let's keep in touch—I'll buy a new cell phone each time," she giggled.

Arthur knew once again that, for a PM, it was impossible to separate business from family affairs. All you could hope for was some stability in one or both areas in order for progress to be made. If both were in chaos then no reasonable politician, let alone a PM, could hope for a measure of effectiveness.

Arthur had not slept much in days. He took a strong brandy and soda, and a copy of *The Oldie* to bed right away and slept until the wee hours. Tomorrow held the promise of a good day, at last.

* * *

Chapter Nine:
Barry Comes Clean

"What the fuck were you thinking?" Beryl yelled at Riggs across the Council committee table. "We are asked to find the computer hackers of Canada's secrets, and it turns out that we are the culprits. Christ!"

"Cool down, Beryl," Barry interjected. "I approved the program of advanced spying by means of computer hacking. I just did not monitor or approve specific operational details. Secretary Riggs, please tell the Council how all of this happened."

"Mr. President, Council members," Riggs replied. "We spent almost five years developing a virus that would breach the firewalls of advanced countries. We successfully penetrated domestic agencies and then a succession of small countries. There were then two necessary steps to take to determine if we had a powerful weapon at our disposal. One was to send it into the computer systems with which we shared some of our top secrets so we could verify our return messages against we already knew we had told the country in question. The other step was to find a small enough, friendly country that would not, like Russia or China, react with hostility when it became apparent that we were operating with knowledge of what they were planning. The selection of Canada was easy. They rely largely on our defence secrets in planning their own defence and foreign policies."

"So how did they discover that their firewalls were all penetrated?" asked Barry. "Perhaps they had some additional, sophisticated monitoring techniques that could signal a successful computer invasion. And they do have a small but expert group of electrical engineers embedded in their top offices, like the Prime Minister's Office."

"Mr. President, we may have to come clean and tell the Prime Minister that we made a very grave mistake," Riggs went on. "The longer we delay the worse it may become."

Beryl interjected, "I disagree," and murmurs of agreement were heard around the room. "I think we will create considerable hostility among our closest allies and, added to that damn hoax about our plans to invade Zimbabwe, our trust quota will have totally disappeared. Let's bluff it out."

"What do you think Sam?" the President asked.

Sam was an unflappable foreign policy advisor who reported exclusively to the President. He had been recruited from the Woodrow Wilson School of Public and International Affairs at Princeton to provide a more traditional information input to that which came from Beryl and her Boy Scout recruits at the State Department.

"I'd say one step at a time," Sam replied. "What is the street knowledge in Ottawa about possible sources? Is the US a suspect? Can we suggest a private sector source of the infiltration, like a WikiLeaks outfit? It could be a successful deflection. But let's review our ambassador's knowledge and that of the Canada desk at State. We know also that Arthur Jones can be a prickly ally."

"A prick!" remarked Beryl.

"Not my favourite," added Evans.

"What do we know about the Zimbabwe hoax right now, Beryl?" asked the President. "Not much," replied Beryl. "There are all kinds of rumours in Ottawa. Most people seem to know that their computer systems were penetrated. Some even allege that the Canadian government was the source of the hoax, but there is no evidence to support that theory. All of the major members of the UN deny any role as a source of the phoney information. Right now we are playing a game with our eyes closed."

Barry was beginning to sense futility in finding the source of the Zimbabwe rumour. He preferred to focus on the most important issue: who infiltrated and destroyed the US defence computer system. He addressed the group directly rather than relying on Riggs.

"We have lost lots of our credibility at home," he began. "I don't want to go on TV for a third time to admit that we have no immediate answers. It is bad enough to make that confession to the Senate foreign relations committee and other Republican activists in the House; saying it on TV only destroys our position further. Our technical people in the Department of Defence and the CIA seem stumped about how the virus got into our system. And again there is little but rumours as to the people behind the invasion. Fortunately, thanks to the support of Russia and Britain in piecing together the common elements of our information technology infrastructure, we have largely recovered our whole system. And of course, the air force was bypassed, on the whole, by the virus so we were not totally defenceless. But it was both awkward and inefficient to keep our troops and navy engaged by means of radio telephone signals. Every teenager in America could listen in to those unencoded transmissions.

"Mr. Vice-President, I'd ask you to reassemble the Senate and House leaders and reassure them we have almost completely restored our full defence capabilities." Ben Levitt nodded agreement to the President.

"Fred, I want you and Sam to meet me daily if not more. For now, we will proceed cautiously, but please be prepared for changes in strategy. And get those darn CIA and FBI people to work even harder, OK?" Evans stood up and made for the exit door. The Council seemed unusually quiet as they gathered their papers and slowly left the room.

* * *

Barry strode back to his private quarters in the White House. He had practised his walk since his first days in the Indiana Statehouse. He felt it improved his image and created the impression of confidence and power. At least Barry thought this from the inside. Others thought he looked like a soldier on parade. No one bothered to tell him either.

Barry was pleased that Debbie, his wife, would not be there. She had shocked a tiny part of Middle America by taking a salaried job with a large Washington law firm. She had grown tired of chairing

NGO committees, visiting the infirm, opening events and tending to the thousands of duties of First Ladies. She was a lawyer by training, specializing in corporate and international law. She missed the intellectual challenges and the sensations of completing a well done brief and case. She phased out most controversial cases when Barry reached the Senate, but felt she kept enough going to retain a measure of sanity. The current job was more particular in thrust as no one wanted her to take cases and be visible in court proceedings. The presidency itself might be compromised or at least threatened with blackmail. So she secured a job doing legal research and preparing notes and case commentaries for a number of the senior partners. They signed off on everything. Debbie gave her salary to her favourite charity and retained only a small expenses budget for a chauffeured limousine and some work clothes in case some commentator would moan about double-dipping.

Debbie was a natural blonde as befitted the descendant of a German immigrant grandfather and an Irish grandmother. She looked a bit like Doris Day, freckles and all, though perhaps a bit faded now. But she was a ruthless woman who held Barry to account for his frequent dalliances. The currency she used came in terms of her personal freedoms. Always a traveller, Debbie would indulge in spur of the moment trips—to the opera in Milan or the baseball tournament in Puerto Rico. Barry could never count on her presence at any formal event. He was smart enough to tell her of the visits of foreign dignitaries though. She hated to miss the chance of meeting foreign royalty from Britain, Spain, Holland and other European countries, which often allowed her to negotiate a return visit. How else was a working girl going to visit the Prada?

Barry always thought they had developed a marriage of convenience. Now he found it a marriage of inconvenience, and he expected the two of them to live apart when he finished his second term in another two years. They had no children or other family complications.

On occasions like the present, Barry always appreciated an opportunity for some consultation and advice. Instead he would put up with silent reflections in his bedroom with a "do-not disturb" request to the security detail posted at the entrance to their apartment.

* * *

As Barry dozed and rethought his problems of governance, he had that intellectual spurt of energy he so wanted. "Darn it," he thought, "I refuse to become the Herbert Hoover of the 21st century. My favourable rating score by the American people went down so quickly, it surely will go up just as fast in the next little while."

Grabbing his jacket, Barry rushed out of his bedroom and apartment and headed for the Oval Office. En route, he stopped at his secretary Lily's desk and asked her to summon Mark Lofthouse from the CIA and Todd Beecham from the FBI. Don't forget Beryl and Fred he reminded himself and Lily. "And get me the Canadian Prime Minister on the phone," he said before entering the office.

Barry very occasionally got a surge of adrenaline. Now was one of those times. They came most frequently before making an important speech or, as he reminded himself, before attempting a seduction and liaison.

Beryl called, "What's up? My secretary said that Lily told her that you were very anxious for me to come over. This isn't the best of times I assure you."

"I need you here ASAP," replied the President. "I am planning to talk to the Canadian Prime Minister and ask him if I can pay an immediate visit. If you can, I'd like you and Fred plus the directors of the CIA and FBI to come too. I want you to hear my discussion with Prime Minister Jones and help me plan my full strategy. I'll wait until you get here and let the others know at the same time."

Lily knocked and entered. "They are all coming over," she said. "But the Prime Minister's office is having some trouble in finding the Prime Minister. He is stressed out by the computer difficulties and now his wife is missing in action. He won't be keen on visitors," she concluded.

* * *

Barry outlined his strategy, at least the elements of a strategy. "We cannot stay put," he began. "We are becoming the laughing stock of the world. And the people behind the virus invasion might be capable of terror against the American people. So this is what I want to do."

"First, I want to go to Canada and admit that our penetration of their top secret computer files was a grievous blunder. And that we want to apologise.

"Second, I want to ask Arthur Jones if he would join us and other NATO allies in declaring war against computer terrorists. Disabling our military computer systems was the same as invasion of our lands. It also put the entire free world at risk of nuclear attack by a rogue government like the one in Iran or Syria.

"Third, I want our FBI and CIA people to come with us and discuss with their Canadian counterparts quite where they are and have been with finding the source of both the hoax and the infiltration of our defence computer systems.

"Fourth, depending on the situation, I will offer Canada some compensation for our blunder such as allowing border traffic without passports at major holiday times like Thanksgiving, Christmas and Easter. And offer to extend these times to weekends throughout the year after a trial period. Any comments?

Most people nodded in agreement. Barry said that only Beryl, Lofthouse and Beecham would comprise their delegation. Once he had got hold of Jones they would schedule a visit before the weekend.

They shuffled out of the Oval Office in silence. Experienced politicians all, they knew to keep silent when the news was good, bad or indifferent. They could smile or frown when responding to the slightest change in the tone of the voice of the speaker. Barry knew this of course. That was one of the reasons he liked Beryl as an ally; pillow-talk was occasionally useful!

* * *

Arthur met the President at the Ottawa Airport. This was unusual protocol, but now he realized that some super effort at ingratiation might prove useful. Both men put on their best smiles, and Arthur smiled at Beryl despite his ingrained contempt for her politics.

The meetings took place on the Hill, almost as soon as the

61

Americans arrived. Barry outlined his position and offered an apology. Arthur, wise to the strategy, accepted without hesitation and without elaboration. He had Raj, Gilles and Tom with him from Cabinet plus Stephen and Richard (CSIS) from the staff side. They all looked quite pleased to be invited.

Arthur agreed that the computer people from CSIS and National Defence needed to work with their US counterparts, and that the Americans should stay over for a couple of days to put together a review of developments as they saw them and then a schedule to deal with the inevitable catalogue of unresolved concerns.

Arthur offered the group a drink and remembered how pleased he was with these developments. After one or two glasses of wine, summoned by Stephen from some unknown place in the PM's outer office, they shook hands and agreed to keep in close touch.

"I wish dealing with family and party caucus could be so satisfactory," Arthur murmured to himself. He remained worried and anxious about Jane. He wished that all of his relationships, political and personal, would enter a new phase now.

Chapter Ten:
Power in Different Places

Jane felt it was now time to contact Arthur directly. She realised that she resented politics, all those meetings, and all that waffle about working for the good of all/families/working families. She had used her patience in good stead to deal with Arthur's ambition and obvious successes. But she knew she was lonely now. No kids at home. Some friends in Ottawa and Victoria, of course, but even with these she must be guarded. Over the past few days, she knew she could not go back without a deal with Arthur. I want him to resign, she thought. He has had his time in the light. I don't want to copy him, but for us to begin a relationship we never really started. Kids and political successes came too fast to develop something deeper.

She reached Arthur at home on Sussex Drive, probably reading executive summaries of PCO documents. "I must come home Arthur," she began.

"And we must talk," he said immediately. "Where are you? Are you OK? We've been worried sick. The RCMP has been no bloody help in finding you." They both needed to settle down.

A full ten seconds passed before Jane said, "I'm catching a red-eye special either tonight or tomorrow. I'd tell you where I am now, but I know your phone is tapped. I have a new cell phone, courtesy of Melanie, who seems to have invested in more than a dozen. Don't tell Gerald I'm coming back."

"I'll plan to be at home tomorrow night and the following night too," Arthur replied. "I'm hoping that we can settle our differences. I had a bit of luck today in that we seem to have entered into a newer, friendly alliance with the Americans. I'm praying my luck will extend to us."

"We need a bit more than luck Arthur. We may need some major shifts in our marriage."

Jane rarely, if ever, spoke so bluntly, and Arthur felt nonplussed. He did not reply. He always had liked a full and frank expression of his thoughts with Jane. Now he did not know whether it was better to open his mouth or to stay totally quiet.

"I can't wait to see you," Jane said, offering some softening words.

"Me too," said Arthur before Jane hung up.

He was hurt and bothered. His favourite swear word was "shit," and the whole house echoed to multiple repeats of that monosyllable both before and when he went to bed.

* * *

Lofthouse and Beecham were staying at the Chateau Laurier. After the President and Secretary of State and their staffers left, they were at a bit of a loss for things to do. Both had been to Ottawa before and found the place civil but uneventful after the commuters left the downtown core. Mark Lofthouse, on the spur of the moment, called Richard at CSIS to ask him over for a drink. "Bring someone from the Mounties too," he asked. At least the guys could swap battle stories of life stuck somewhere between the politicians, their public servants and operatives, and those suspicious enemy agents. At these kinds of gatherings, the truth was well massaged and the people well characterized.

Richard showed up with Gerald, whom the Americans did not know. "I couldn't find Gilbert (the RCMP Commissioner)," he added. "He's probably in Gatineau playing cards with his wife's family," he smirked.

Richard loved to play "I'm better than you" with all of his colleagues. He did not go to private school for no reason.

Mark began by teasing Richard about Ottawa and its missing football team. "First they go bankrupt and second, you can't organize a replacement," he began. He amplified, "The CFL is a league of NFL castoffs, especially those who will work for less than 100K per season." Neither Richard nor Gerald looked amused. But Gerald had to say, "And the best American hockey players have first names like

Jeremy or Travis, because their mothers wanted girls." That brought only groans and an offer to buy more beers.

"Love Canadian beer," declared Mark. "Anything new in those parts except this computer crisis"

Richard said, "That bitch, the PM's wife, went walkabout about a week ago, and Gerald and his colleagues couldn't be bothered to find her."

"She'll come back," Gerald said. "She is having another midlife crisis. Probably wants the old man to retire to Salt Spring Island."

"Where the hell is that?" interjected Todd Beecham.

"Oh, out there on the west coast, between Vancouver and Vancouver Island. It has a population of about 5000, many with long grey hair and Birkenstock sandals they bought in 1965," retorted Richard. "But I like the place. It doesn't snow all the time like Ottawa in the winter."

"We are fed up with keeping an eye on Jane Jones," said Gerald. "She gives us the slip and we get shit from upstairs for not doing our jobs. And our hands are tied, as we are under orders not to be too obtrusive. So I'm happy she has disappeared to somewhere in BC, we think. She'll be back soon—mark my words."

Mark observed, "You are very casual, you Canadians. That's what I like about you."

"Little do you know," Richard remarked with a smile. "Arthur Jones can be a real terrorist himself. At least that is what the rumours suggest. He likes to organise opposition coalitions and, now that he is the PM, he gets to organise them in the international arena. No one is immune, including the US. Cocky bastard."

Mark and Todd were silent. "Go on," said Mark.

"Not much to go on about," said Richard. "Ottawa is full of rumours. Gerald probably knows more than I do, don't you Gerald?"

* * *

Jane thought she had made a mistake in coming home when her plane touched down in the wee morning hours. All she could see ahead was an argument with Arthur, a day alone looking through correspondence and then an evening spent largely by herself while Arthur read from his dispatch box. One day was OK, two even understandable, but days on end quite debilitating. She could visit or call friends but, like many spouses, she felt intrusive as the lonely wife in a larger gathering. Funny how one could be lonely amidst a crowd.

The weather was damp and grey, with hints of sleet. The taxi driver, like many in Ottawa, was Lebanese which gave him, if we are to believe Jane, full insights to curse at Arthur and his government. She offered no reply. Just get me there, she thought. He finally shut up when he realized he was heading towards Sussex Drive. He even looked a little scared. Jane thought that was a first. He had probably bullied many of the women in his life, besides his mother. Perhaps multiple wives held simultaneously curbed his anger and resentments, she thought. Pity that bigotry was not a criminal offence in Canada.

Arthur had left a note under the jar of Robertson's marmalade in the kitchen. "Call me immediately at the PMO," it said. "I'll come right over. Stephen and Denise (Arthur's Parliamentary Secretary) can hold the fort."

Jane felt he could wait awhile. She trudged upstairs, stripped in the bathroom and soaked herself in the tub. Her muscles needed relaxation after being cooped up on a plane for five hours. She looked forward to her breakfast reading the paper. Then she'd phone Arthur, damn him.

* * *

Arthur was in fact in Anne's office soaking up some strong loving which he had sorely missed in recent years. Anne was immensely energetic and wanted multiple orgasms which Arthur tried to oblige. They were lying on the carpeted floor, with Arthur's head almost beneath her desk and Anne smiling down at him with a look of something close to devotion.

They finally got up and vowed to keep repeating this performance in future days. Arthur reminded Anne of the dangers of a scandal to all concerned and to his capacities to finance his daughters' university education. They staggered their departures from Anne's office.

By the time Arthur returned to the PMO, Jane had called and reminded him to come home for lunch and a heart-to-heart talk. Arthur knew it was essential that much of the rest of his life should have that kind of intensity.

He just had a few minutes to get Stephen to brief him on the morning's events. He needed some prep time after lunch to answer questions regarding new negotiations with First Nations communities about the significance of official recognition of the aboriginal government as a co-equal third level. There were a host of constitutional ramifications in making this gesture, particularly involving the Federal Crown's fiduciary obligations, as well as policy impacts on land claims negotiations. Arthur was always in a dilemma about symbolic politics. He disliked flags, bands, parades, resolutions in Parliament, renaming of mountains and islands. But he also liked approval from the variety of interests and of individuals across the country. It was, he thought, the classic battle between the left and right brains of the country. Rationality vs. emotionalism.

Stephen advised the PM to go slowly on the issue. Few people in Canada understood the dilemma, and not many MPs wanted a constitutional debate notwithstanding that many were trained lawyers. The PM also knew that many voters disliked constitutional change and felt unease at full reconciliation with First Nations. Many of the seats his party had picked up in the Prairies and in Northern Ontario had a history of racism. Arthur also knew that waffle in Parliament would satisfy no one. No, he thought, I need some direct statements with clear steps and timelines for moving the process along. The dangers of not meeting deadlines were relatively small compared with the dangers of stalling. Stephen agreed to meet with Denise and draft a statement for Question Period. George Conway, the Minister, would be all for this strategy, and Stephen suggested they ask a backbencher from Quebec to pose a question to the Minister. Arthur would reply on any supplementary question. Nobody needed to know for sure what the opposition parties wanted.

Arthur rushed to his limousine, pulling his overcoat on as he went. He had less than five minutes to focus on the few points he needed to emphasize in his discussion with Jane. He also knew that he would probably have to proceed with instinct rather than forethought.

Jane greeted him at the door with a big hug and a peck on the cheek before waving at Gordon, their driver.

* * *

Gerald respected the Prime Minister. Gerald respected people in authority. He had respected his dad too, an RCMP officer whose career in rural Alberta was defined by unshakeable integrity and respect from rural folk and aboriginal band councillors alike. Gerald believed his dad was the real government in those parts and in those days. He felt that order was the glue for a fragmented society of multiple ethnicities, for even just two ethnic groups like English and French. And order could only come from respect for those in authority, from the Prime Minister and Premiers down to the front-line police officers.

He was quite upset with the challenge of Richard's question. He loved dealing with fellow professional lawmen, even if they were in the spy business. He also loved the camaraderie of law officers on both sides of the Canada–US border. They shared similar problems albeit on a greater scale in the many large US cities.

But Gerald did not want to betray his Prime Minister by inadvertently passing along information he had overheard in the corridors of Parliament or the Prime Minister's Office. Like Arthur, he struggled to find the right course of action.

"Well, there are lots of rumours flying about. I know from talking with CSIS people like Richard that we are all upset at having our computer systems hacked by Washington. It makes no sense to us. I hope that now the President has apologised we can get back to cordial times. What else should I say, Richard?" asked Gerald.

Richard added, "We also know, as do you guys, that we have no idea of the source of the hoax that was played regarding the invasion of Zimbabwe. We were and are stumped on that, and our top levels of government just as insulted as other leaders about the issue."

Mark Lofthouse smiled as he said, "You guys are no good. We

come all the way to Ottawa for some decent gossip and we get none. The only thing of remote interest is the news that the Prime Minister's wife went on a holiday to BC, all by herself, I gather. Not very juicy."

"Don't worry," said Gerald. "She will be back tomorrow, I'm told. Obviously wants the old man to retire and he is barely 60 years old. He actually loves politics and likes the voters. He'll stay even if she retires to Victoria with all the other geriatrics. And there are lots of other smart looking women on his backbench who would love to be one of the PM's partners instead. We are all pretty open-minded about these things in Canada."

After a short silence, Richard asked the Americans for any new developments on the hacking into their military computers. When he said new developments, he actually meant today's developments as he was in frequent touch with Lofthouse and others in Washington.

Lofthouse grumbled about the current strategy. "We've been spending time trying to isolate those groups and governments who might wish to do us harm, but I believe the hackers may simply be clever people unconnected with previous computer crimes. If I'm right then it makes our job more complicated."

After some silence, Gerald said, "We'd better go. See you tomorrow."

The two departed, and as Lofthouse closed the door behind them, he remarked ,"Interesting stuff about the PM's wife. I wonder if she has hacker friends in BC? Best if we consider options. But by orders ourselves and not with the RCMP."

Chapter Eleven:
Family Ties?

Arthur was sitting in an aisle seat in executive class on a flight from Ottawa to Vancouver. Jane sat next to him in the window seat. He had three "guardians" or "minders" with him. Gerald sat across the aisle, one Mountie sat in front of Arthur and another behind him. They formed a small diamond shape, Arthur mused.

He always felt awkward using executive class. He loved meeting people, even on planes, but the great "washed" Canadian public never gave up lobbying him for an instant. The five-hour trip in peace also gave him some time to catch up on the infernal memos that Stephen pushed through to him or that sometimes came directly from members of the Cabinet. When they got to Vancouver, one of the Mounties would immediately catch the red-eye special back to Ottawa, carrying the approved documents and recommendations. Jane, he and Gerald would get a helicopter to the Victoria harbour. "All expensive stuff," Gerald said to himself.

Arthur found it difficult to focus on the paperwork. He and Jane were using the opportunity of the late February week's break in Parliament to fly home to work out their respective concerns with the marriage. Jane felt more concerned than Arthur as he was always called upon to mend fences and catch up with details during this week. Now he worried about his work–life balance, a concept he hated since the time he had to fire a lazy executive assistant at the beginning of his political career. She used the principle as an excuse for laziness, and he had distrusted the word since that time.

Arthur also doubted that he and Jane would agree on a way to rebuild their relationship, at least within a week at home. It would at best yield a protocol or a partial framework, in his terms. He shuddered at the idea of using political jargon to understand his marriage. His deeper side feared the worst. He had always been a pessimist who took some courage from occasional success. He couldn't play tennis or squash or any other game without believing he would lose. He felt the same way about his relationship with Jane. He would lose even though he knew it wasn't a contest. It was a foreboding, melancholy personality, assuaged only by the prospect and thrill of political work. And, he must admit, by the acclamation and approval of others.

Jane wanted to know what he was working on. He told her he was reading a series of executive summaries on northern mining projects in BC, Ontario and Quebec. They needed no approval or disapproval at this stage and he was not inclined to stifle any initiative by the private sector. He employed thousands of cautious public servants to point out the difficulties.

Jane wanted to talk, it seemed, so he felt it necessary to set aside his papers for a short break. She looked remarkably happy, perhaps because she had persuaded them to take a bit of a break. Arthur warned her that he'd need to check in with the PMO on a daily basis, and his innate pessimism made him think of various crises around the country and world. He forced himself back to the reality of conversation.

"Do you really think we should buy something new?" he asked Jane.

Jane had suggested they stop living in a furnished suite in Victoria in order to invest in a retirement home. It reversed their previous status. They had had a serviceable three-bedroom home with a finished basement in the Saanich panhandle before Arthur went to Ottawa, but discovered that renters were never very reliable and home upkeep was expensive even on the PM's salary. They had become renters themselves, in the PM's residence in Ottawa (no charge), and in a two-bedroom furnished unit on Humboldt Street in downtown Victoria.

"I want to settle down," said Jane, now in her late fifties like Arthur. "I've missed so much of a normal person's life, with meetings and receptions and conferences and you off to various parts of the country and world. Let's chill out."

Arthur agreed with all of that. But he knew he needed more stimulation in his life than that offered to an aging but popular ex-prime minister. He didn't want any honorary degrees or accolades that he did not directly earn. And his golf was terrible too. For some unaccountable reason he thought of Anne. He would miss her terribly. He knew how lust would destroy so much in his life—his marriage and his parliamentary respect. He needed to put her at the very back of his mind, especially this week. He wondered whether Gerald and colleagues knew about his liaisons with Anne. They were always great at discovering scandals at home that involved sexual rather than state secrets. And Gerald was the kind of card player who would accumulate trumps for a future play in the game.

Both Arthur and Jane settled back into silence. Arthur resumed his paperwork. Jane browsed through the video offerings on the seat back in front of her. Settling on a romantic comedy, Jane seemed absorbed. Arthur was determined to complete his tasks before they landed in Vancouver. Everyone seemed in a torpor even the crew.

The time to land came quickly for the Jones'. Gerald looked pleased and organized the crew to let the PM and his wife and minders off the plane first. It only cost an autograph by Arthur of some photos of him that his office liked. Arthur loved that. If this is the price of public office, Arthur thought, then make me PM forever.

* * *

Jane opened their discussion over breakfast in Victoria the following morning. "I need you to resign and to commit to a normal relationship with me over again." Her opening statements in any arguments with Arthur were never accommodating. She liked to stake out her position and let him react. Normally he did, without reservation. Trouble was his temperament rebelled against direct requests like that.

"We can't do that," he replied. "In any scenario it would take some time to wind up affairs in Ottawa and develop plans for a new life. Besides, politics is my life. I will agree to a transition, a phasing out but not a radical reversal."

Jane then played her trump card, totally unexpected by Arthur.

"You need to know that I'm prepared to leak the information that you and your cronies in Cabinet are the forces of evil that US security is seeking."

Arthur was stunned.

Jane went on, "You told me everything and I'll use it against you if you don't come to reason. Thirty or more years in politics are enough for you and for me."

"Jane you cannot do this to me," replied Arthur. "We have always shared secrets and in this case we shared a critical political secret. Not more than half a dozen people know of my deal with Israel, and not many more outside the security establishment know of my virus attack on the Pentagon. If you leak these things, not only I but the whole country will be scandalized domestically and in the eyes of the world."

"I was thinking a lot about our relationship when I was on Cortes Island," replied Jane. "I concluded that the status quo or even the status quo with a few changes is insufficient. We need a radical restart. You could survive the political scandal. You are a tough bugger, Arthur, and I love you. But I'm not loving you anymore at the price you exact from me. Sorry!"

Arthur was still in his robe and pyjamas. Wandering to the window he could see the Olympic Mountain range, so majestic to the south.

"What if I told the tabloids like the *Sun* that you took off to Cortes Island to stay with an old friend and drove your husband and family to distraction? What would you say to that?"

"That's so trivial, Arthur. Is that the best you can do? Besides I've heard the rumours about you and Anne. I can leak those too if you'd like."

"My God, Jane," said Arthur. "All of this thrown at me at breakfast time. What makes you so angry? I know I have done some things in my career and personal life that you do not like, but I never thought you would resort to using them against me, destroying me. Why did you want to come here? This is no new start for me or for you."

"I need your serious attention," was Jane's response.

73

"More than that," replied Arthur. "You want blood and guts too. How can we ever repair our relationship after your threats of potential exploitation?"

"Think about it," said Jane. "Gerald and Stephen know of your philandering, and there are lots of aspiring prime ministers in your Cabinet who are spreading rumours about you, false or not. Get with the programme old man. Who is exploiting whom?"

Arthur left the breakfast room and started his ablutions. He could not think straight. Betrayal by his wife was never one of his fears. Betrayal by a colleague was always a possibility in politics. What could she want, besides his destruction? A shave and shower helped him develop some kind of strategy, one to get him through the next few hours at least.

* * *

Beryl and Barry were at Beryl's small apartment. Every Monday, they enjoyed a "nooner" followed by a review of key issues from the week. They found it easier to talk strategy and tactics in the tranquility of post-coital bliss than in the noise and interruptions of the Oval Office.

Eventually Barry brought up their trip to Ottawa. "Went off well," he asserted. "Arthur is a grand host and the Canadian MPs very receptive to genuine gestures of friendship." Beryl did not respond.

Eventually, she murmured, "He is a bit too Ivy League for my taste, at least in terms of style." Arthur would have been appalled if he had heard her characterization. "And his wife is a woman who smiles with her mouth and never with her eyes."

"I'm surprised you came to that conclusion," Barry said, reaching down her body to stroke her vulva. "She came across to me as a bit of a flirt but one very much in charge of Arthur, poor guy."

"I can't do it again, Barry," said Beryl. "We need to get out of here soon. And, you need to pay more attention to the Canada file. There are rumours in Ottawa that Canada was a source of or at least a conduit for the hackers into our defence system. We have our CIA men there right now working with the RCMP, and our sources tell us to pay particular attention to the PM's wife. She was brought up on Vancouver Island with a lot of draft dodgers and other kooks, and can espouse all kinds of weird causes. She seems to have developed a taste for running off without telling her family where she can be found."

"We have people looking into this?" Barry responded.

"Many," was Beryl's reply. "We have strong working relationships with their security people and police, and for a small country they are exceptionally large in numbers and scope of their files."

"Keep me up to date, Beryl," said Barry. "Don't worry about Riggs and protocol. I like to work directly with key politicians as you know."

Barry was referring to his presidential style. He wasn't an Eisenhower who thought he was running an army led by generals. He wasn't a "W" who left most operational matters to his vice-president. He was a bit like FDR, Barry thought. Someone who developed critical networks and clusters of policy concerns, such as foreign affairs, defence and security, or socio-economic domestic issues. He had a trusted confidante in each of the clusters he had formed and attempted to meet weekly with three or four of them. They were always informal; only the meetings with Beryl came with "benefits." Barry's biggest problem with his governance networks was his lust for sins of the flesh, both sexual and digestive. Last-minute temptations could always divert him from an appointed task. He seemed to need love and approval in all its forms from everyone he met. Cabinet secretaries played along with this game.

"Can we get someone to work on the Mrs. Jones' factor from the west coast perspective? Someone new Someone without formal ties to our government. An American living in Vancouver perhaps

"I'll see what I can do," said Beryl who had finished dressing. "Get up and get out of here you shagger. And Barry got up and got out of there, albeit with a moment or two of interruptions to get dressed.

* * *

By the time Arthur shuffled out to the living room, Jane had gone, leaving a note on the table. "Gone across the road to St. Ann's gardens with one of my new cell phones. I want to call Dave Bond on Cortes. I imagine this place is bugged so I'll keep walking around trees in the garden just to annoy any long-distance surveillance."

Arthur smiled and thought, "That's the old Jane, not this new kind of terrorist."

He plopped into a comfy chair and began a list of things to say to Jane. He was normally good at conflict resolution but he knew that family conflicts, for him, aroused passions he disliked—anger, rhetoric, sarcasm, even revenge. He also found that compiling a list of items to talk about helped in both domestic and professional contexts. He rarely followed the order of items but preferred to let conversation flow as if nothing he said seemed to be thought through.

Jane returned in less than ten minutes, grumbling that Dave was not at home. His voicemail said "gone fishing" according to Jane. Jane allowed that Dave never announced whether he was fishing or not. For Cortes Islanders, it was equivalent to announcing that one was doing a wash, a routine but necessary task. Arthur merely smiled at the analogy.

"Can we talk a bit now, Jane?" Arthur began. "Shall we talk here in front of the bugs or go for a stroll along Dallas Road? I'd prefer the latter."

"I realize you have a formidable array of weapons," began Arthur, "but I am shocked that you would consider using them so suddenly and against me. I'm devastated."

Jane kept silent before confessing, "I have no way to influence your lifestyle, your behaviour, your choice of friends, and your timetable. Even your constituency visits are getting rare, leaving me a choice between tea with some unknown ambassador's wife or a drink with an uppity woman senator who needs some calming down. The girls are essentially on their own now. The only choices we have are a new career for me, under-qualified in any trade except smiling, and the chance for us both to come home and develop our own business or source of fun."

"You make an excellent case," Arthur replied. "I have worried about your options for some time. But can we work on the second option and get some advice from friends in both Ottawa and Victoria as to opportunities here, and then create a timetable for my withdrawal from electoral politics. We've talked before about ten years being a maximum term in office, and I'm already eight years in. I'd feel better with a timetable, better for us and for the Party as it chooses a new leader."

"Can I trust you Arthur?" Jane wanted to know. "You are very much your own person. Shit! I'll give you until June next year. That's enough time to schedule a new leadership conference in the late fall and let you work through the budget and a few meetings like the Commonwealth Prime Ministers Conference in Colombo. I've always wanted to visit Sri Lanka."

Arthur wanted to challenge Jane. How was it that she set the agenda? He always set the agenda and used its ordering and timing and construction to glide into favoured positions. Instead, Arthur said "OK, with two caveats. First, drop the blackmail about the computer hacking. Second, give me a month or two of flexibility around the dates. Can you live with those?"

Jane replied, "I can live with the second one, but I'll never surrender the first. It is the only power I have. Love doesn't conquer all after thirty or so years."

"Then can I trust you Jane?" Arthur replied to her earlier question. "We need a timetable and process to wind down our Ottawa operations."

"When we get back, I'll try Dave again," was Jane's only reply.

* * *

Chapter Twelve: Owning Up a Bit

Dave stood on the upland of the beach in front of his small home. The cold north-eastern wind could easily keep him indoors at this time of year. But Stella his retriever had needs too, and occasionally they both satisfied their needs in the secure knowledge there was no one within ten miles who could ever see the contented pair.

Stella was restless. She could detect noise easily and she now paced the beach emitting the occasional yelp. Dave too was able to sense something different as the seagulls seemed to be restless above the forested land behind his house. He hoped that no one was visiting. Locals always came by boat, and Dave always went shopping by boat and ferry to Campbell River via Mudge Island. His pick-up was parked at the ferry dock. Now Dave guessed that his visitors, probably two of them judging by the noise, were hiking along the trail that harboured the electrical line from the main road about half an hour away.

Dave never took kindly to newcomers visiting his hideaway. He was happy to meet new people on Vancouver Island, but not here. Hideaways were hideaways in his mind. And he could hear the voices of two men, one American judging from his accent. He strolled back to his house and waited for the knock, allowing Stella the luxury of a twenty-second bark to send a deliberate message to the strangers.

"Hi," announced one of the strangers, a tall blonde man about 45 years old. "I'm Brian Eddy and my friend here is Mark Lofthouse from the States. We are looking for property in this part of the Gulf Islands for some small-scale developments. We know the minimum size is ten acres by regulation of the Island's government. So we need to think of multiple units in specialized tourist or recreational facilities. We want your opinion in part on locations but largely on community feelings. Is it possible for us to work with residents of the Island to develop our concept? The taxes that our venture would pay could fund many Island projects. We think that if the Island residents look favourably on us, we could move to the next step and get the government on side."

Dave looked stunned. He had heard a lot of BS in his days, but no one with an iota of brain cells would look at developing recreational property on this remote island. Many people in Victoria had lost capital in developments there in the past, and those locations were accessible by car and ferry. Success on Cortes would require something like a posh marina or a helicopter pad he felt. And the people with the cash to come would probably prefer to buy and build their own hideaway cottages. He immediately wondered what was the real agenda of these two middle-aged men

"This is a wonderful place for people to come and visit or live," he began. "But people here are very protective of their environment. They don't like outsiders either."

The silence seemed endless before Dave's cell phone rang. He did not answer it and waited instead for a response from his visitors. He always found that the patience to live with silence for minutes or more was a good negotiating strategy. Many people could not endure silence and broke it with comments that compromised their positions. So all three, funnily enough, sat in silence, each waiting for someone else to yield.

Dave got up and, patting Stella, said, "I'm sorry you are not getting the reaction you seemed to want. I'm busy. Would you please go now?"

The two visitors showed no signs of leaving. Finally, Lofthouse said, "We want to know why you seem to be in touch with the wife of the Prime Minister. The US as a major ally needs reliable friends, and we worry about the reliability of the Canadian PM, his wife and his family. Why are you dabbling with Jane Jones? Is this an affair or something of political concern to our two countries?"

"Bugger off," was Dave's first comment. He opened the door letting in some chill air. "Jane and I and Arthur are great old friends going back a generation. You did not need to come here to find this out."

"We would like you to come with us now," replied Brian. "I'm an RCMP officer. Here's my badge. We have grounds to believe that you and Jane are plotting some kind of conspiracy, perhaps with others, to undermine our governments and their defences. We have a helicopter on call. It can be here in half an hour."

Dave took off with Stella, commanding her to get the visitors as they chased. Dave knew that a near senior citizen could not outrun two obviously fit cops. But he knew the terrain and how to out-circle the invaders. He hoped that Stella would keep them at bay. The sound of a gunshot made him think that hope was a gamble.

* * *

Arthur was early. He sat at a table along with Stephen and Raj. They faced Gary Prevost, the Chair of the House committee on foreign affairs and defence. Gary was perhaps eighteen to twenty feet away from Arthur. The whole committee had yet to assemble at the tables that formed a large square of meeting space. The venue was the Confederation Room in the East Block, a large somnolent space in corridors filled with moving anxious people. The room accommodated perhaps 100 people, seated in rows behind Arthur so he did not have to wave and recognize them.

Arthur was rarely early. He loved to squeeze out an extra five minutes with someone before he ran into a staffer who desperately needed one or two more. And a gregarious politician could only love the altercation and drama of constant change.

After three months of stalling, Arthur had finally agreed to discuss his role in the hacking scandal, now known in Ottawa as "computergate" Raj had met with the Committee a couple of times as had Gilles. The media pressure, Opposition noises, and caucus questions finally induced Arthur to testify. He loved the full Parliament where he could engage in debates and Question Period and let loose his clever, often acid, wit. He disliked committees given the uncertainty of the questions. He knew that an innocent statement or comment could escalate. And the TV would show every grimace and smile in response.

Arthur had met with Gary on a number of occasions both before and since he had become Prime Minister. He had thought that Gary could make a grand contribution to Cabinet. Gary thought otherwise. "I love Parliament," was Gary's statement, "but I hate those well-mannered creeps who staff the executive class of the public service. Never a straight answer. Always a yes and a no to a question. Always a disguise to cover up the implementation boondoggles. No, not that for me. Besides I like my weekends in Toronto at home, watching the Leafs and cheering for Upper Canada College's football team." Arthur and Gary settled on this job, which meant that someone in the position could be offended. Arthur reflected on the double-edged sword of his patronage, of how a reward for one could become a rejection of the other. He was never persuaded to bureaucratize his patronage. He loved discretion, even power, and hated mindless rules designed to address historical problems.

Gary and Arthur met some weeks before Arthur's appearance. There were scheduling difficulties to resolve, and they each wanted "a word" in advance. Arthur wanted a quick move around the table of assembled politicians, limiting supplementary questions. Gary wanted to show how astute questions could bring forth astute answers from this exemplary first minister, so he agreed to strict time limits for the buccaneers on the committee. No appeals, no excuses. Ten minutes per person and no limits on Arthur's opening statements.

Arthur began with the necessary platitudes. "Thank you Mr. Chairman. How pleased I am to be here. This is what democracy is all about. A time for people and their representatives to share information and to debate its implications—without rumour, without jealousy and without personal ambitions. Committees such as these are ideal for this kind of discussion, and this committee plays a pivotal role in Canadian democracy as it deals with issues involving our place in the world and the professionalism with which we resolve them.

"I am very glad that some of my Cabinet colleagues have been able to talk to you on previous occasions. They know fully the sequence of events that ensued after some organization or government or individual hacked into our entire computer systems. We know now that some rogue clients in the US establishment experimented with their skills at hacking and treated us, their closest allies, as laboratory matter. President Evans has fully and publicly apologized as you know. But the US has also been subject to hacking and its defences have been compromised, at least potentially. We gather from US defence authorities that their systems are now fully operational. I believe you know most if not all of these events and much of the background since it all began.

"I must state now, in an unequivocal way, that I cannot, as the Prime Minister of this great country, neglect to secure our information systems and our defences. We have restructured our computer networks and firewalls. We are working with the Americans and other allies to discover how, when and where the hackers got loose.

"For your reference, I have had my staff produce a summary of events surrounding these incidents. They have also identified the key agencies and personnel that individual members can access for the most recent information. We will be happy to provide more written information if members of this committee so desire.

"I say to you: what we have experienced is devastating to our self-regard. But what we have experienced since has been a grand awareness and a grand set of methods to guarantee the security of this nation and of its citizens. Thank you for inviting me here to demonstrate your awareness and concern. God bless Canada."

Arthur could not figure where he got that last statement. It was not in his notes. There were lots of hostile atheists in Canada. He admired the capacity of American presidents to invoke supreme powers on their behalf. Damn it, he needed that, in the later cool of day.

The questions began, going clockwise around the table. The members were all excruciatingly polite and a touch deferential. Arthur loved it. He could enter into that kind of language and ethos. He had no difficulty in keeping part of his history of these events tucked away safely at the back of his mind. As soon as these questions touched on potentially difficult issues, Arthur resorted to agreeing with the intent of the questions. "Yes, we have thought about that problem." "Yes we have consulted our NATO allies and they have shared their expertise." "Yes, you raise an important issue that we must address in the PMO and in Parliament itself." Arthur felt a bit like Sir Humphrey, the famous character in the BBC TV series "Yes Minister" and "Yes, Prime Minister."

About half way around the table, the members began to wilt visibly. They realized that nothing new would be forthcoming today. Gary summed up feelings at the end.

"We are very grateful you could find the time to update us on these issues, and we hope you will continue to keep us informed as investigations proceed. Thank you, Prime Minister."

Arthur regarded Gary as a consummate chair and friend of the governing party. He reminded himself to consult him further on other issues.

On the way out of the room, Arthur caught sight of Anne. She winked. He reciprocated with a smile. In politics, he thought, you would never have too many loyal friends. Too many dangerous people lurked in every caucus.

* * *

Jane had sneaked into the committee room virtually unnoticed, and sat in the back corner almost obscured from the politicians and their tables at the front. Arthur did not know that she planned to come, although he liked it when she attended meetings at which he performed. Her comments were constructive, sometimes critical and sometimes praiseworthy.

This time she was in complete admiration of his rhetoric, his body language and (almost) of the content of his talk. It was nostalgic too, reminding her of his first run at electoral office as a twenty-something in Victoria, BC. She felt a twinge of seduction, which was remarkable after almost fifty years as friend, lover and wife.

Near the end of the talk, Jane recalled Dave's words as she left Cortes Island for Ottawa: "Arthur will get through all of this. He has the ability to speak the whole truth about an issue or a problem and do so in the sincerest way. But he has perfected the technique of neglecting any linkages in his mind with topics he wants to avoid. A quick brain and a facile tongue let him slide past or over or around chosen issues. Be careful about him, dear Jane," Dave continued. "He may be speaking just some of the whole truth with you."

Those words had stayed with her. They altered her understanding of and feelings about Arthur. It was as if she had been told about an adulterous affair, out of the blue, in an exposed group of people.

She stopped into Arthur's office on her way back to 24 Sussex. She knew most if not all of the executive assistants who worked with Stephen on Parliament Hill. There was another group who worked in a high-rise on Slater Street, just five minutes' walk away. They mostly handled the mail, the emails and the questions from home and abroad. Important communications were downloaded onto a USB stick and walked over to the "inner circle" offices. It took those employees over six weeks to learn which kind of form response went to which kind of person, and which person was to be considered "important" and which was not. All constituency matters were sent immediately to Arthur's 2-I-C located in Victoria for an immediate response and perhaps a visit too if necessary. Arthur had a great deal of faith in his assistants, and Stephen met a high standard of performance that others had to try valiantly to emulate. Arthur thought it rather amusing that the CIA knew the names and curricula vitae of over 600 people, most of whom would have absolutely no knowledge of the grand affairs of the state.

Jane asked one of the assistants near the office door if Arthur was busy. The assistant replied, "Yes, he is making a series of phone calls to the premiers to finalize the agenda for the so-called economic summit scheduled for early July." Jane felt a little piqued, which amplified her concerns about Arthur and the other spheres of his life in which he operated.

She checked herself and said, "Please tell him to call me at home this afternoon. We need to chat."

Arthur finally called at about 6 pm, explaining about how his ears always hurt when the Quebec Premier spoke. "It never seems to be in French or in English, but rather a mix of the two," moaned Arthur.

"We need to discuss our arrangement for your resignation again," began Jane. "Can we do it after dinner?"

"Why?" replied Arthur. "I have lots of reading to catch up on."

"Yes I thought so," Jane commented. "But I want us to agree on actual dates rather than target times. Not everything can be made precise but you too need to fit everything into your public schedule."

"I guess," said Arthur before hanging up.

* * *

It did not take long for Arthur and Jane to agree on dates. Arthur had only two concerns. He needed to give the Party some months' notice, in part so they could revamp the policy conference scheduled at the Royal York for the week after Thanksgiving. It was to be transformed into a national arena for the leadership candidates, one week prior to the electronic balloting process. Electronic balloting was becoming the norm and it gave all members a chance to participate in choosing Arthur's successor from their own homes. A trip to Toronto was too expensive for many members.

Arthur's second concern reflected his underlying vanity, rarely expressed but triggered for all kinds of reasons at unpredictable times. Arthur wanted the national press and TV networks to write up a well-considered and accurate review of his time in office and his contributions to the country. So he persuaded Jane to accept the idea of publicly announcing his resignation a week or so before a slow news weekend like the Victoria Day holiday in May. He might also give his local paper in Victoria a scoop on the day he would be announcing his resignation on TV.

Arthur agreed to Jane's only previous demand, that they could spend the whole summer in Victoria and settle on a new home. He would need to resign in early June and ask the deputy prime minister to act in his stead for up to six months. The Cabinet could run smoothly under his laissez faire approach to decision making, and the House could be kept busy with a pile of housekeeping bills that were always ready to be passed but often got squeezed out of the available time. They would all have to hope that no new crisis would emerge requiring clear, strategic leadership.

Arthur remarked that he would tell Stephen tomorrow, and he'd call Vera, the lead coordinator in his Victoria office, immediately after that. From there he would tell the Party hierarchy and the Cabinet. An announcement in Parliament would provide a good chance for him to practise his farewell address at the convention itself.

Both Jane and Arthur felt well pleased with their discussions. A schedule had been established. Jane would tell the kids that night but use their secret codes to get them both to call on new cell phones well away from their rooms.

"Oops," was Arthur's final remark before he went back to the Hill. "I forgot. I'll have to advise the Governor General too! Funny how we forget the monarchy and one of its few important functions of government."

Chapter Thirteen: Playing for Keeps

Arthur dreaded the prospect of telling Anne about his decision to resign. It meant that, for all practical purposes, they would be living 4000 kilometres apart. He had come to rely on Anne's good sense, her rectitude and especially her loving. She made him feel like a young man or, as she put it, "a young studley"

On his return to Parliament Hill after discussing his schedule of resignation with Jane, Arthur went straight to Anne's office. She was not there, but her executive assistant said she would be back in a few moments and asked Arthur if he would prefer to wait in her private office. Arthur said he had best not wait. On his way to the door, Anne burst in and greeted him warmly but literally at arm's length.

He told her of his plans as soon as they sat together on the couch in her office. She looked forlorn, even abandoned.

"How can I see you now?" she asked. "It would mean leaving Ottawa on a late Thursday plane and confining our get-togethers to Fridays in Vancouver."

He put his arms around her and she snuggled on his chest. Her free hand reached down and unzipped his fly with deliberate care.

"I want to stay together," said Anne as she grasped his penis. "Can we?"

"I don't really see how," said Arthur. "I'm twenty years older than you and you'll be a widow in twenty some years. I feel I must stay loyal to Jane given all she has given up to be by my side." He went on, "But I want to remain your lover, even if our loving becomes irregular."

Anne lowered her head and let her tears drop onto his exposed member. She licked as well until he became unusually wet, and then she used hand and mouth to his delight. She paused to swallow, then got up to straighten her hair in mirror behind the door.

"Damn you, Arthur. I wasn't supposed to fall in love. You were to be my passionate combination of lust and power. Now I've lost the lust and have little power."

"We've got a couple of months to figure things out," said Arthur. "We'll find a way to meet regularly, unless of course we grow apart due to location and work commitments. I'll need to find some work on the west coast; some paying directorships might be needed."

"Meet me tomorrow, Arthur. Please! My apartment, come during Question Period. No one will miss us. Only Gilles will notice that we are both absent. Gilles may know we are an item anyway. He has a network of contacts among the staff who work in MPs' offices or provide security on site."

"What if we do lunch instead, Anne? I'll cancel my arrangements. They are probably to talk to someone from the exporter's council about expanded free trade into South America. That can wait. I want to be in the House for Question Period. I actually try to learn about the agenda of politics from the character of questions advanced by the backbenchers. I know they are filtered through the whips' offices, but over time one can get a different feel than is provided by surveys, encounter groups or even messages from individual citizens."

"I must go," said Anne. "Damn you again, Arthur." They left her office separately in their usual fashion.

"Another office, another orgasm," Arthur thought to himself.

* * *

Jane went to her local gym at least three times a week. She preferred the gym at the University of Ottawa, both because she could walk there and because the other clients did not seem to recognise her. She enrolled in a one-semester course and paid her student dues in order to get access to the facilities. She liked feeling fit, and she had managed to keep a relatively slender figure.

She tried to go before breakfast, around 7 am. At that time, Arthur was both grumpy and obsessed with the news of the new day. He had the Times-Colonist (Victoria) on his laptop, the CBC on his portable radio, and hard copies of the *Toronto*, the *Globe* and the *Montreal Gazette*. He didn't pretend to take much in. He anxiously skimmed the papers and tuned into CBC news for critical events and comments. When he got to his office at about 8:30 am, he would be handed a hard-copy synopsis of the previous day's events. Stephen was also ready with any important news that was breaking or had arisen since the previous day.

Though she preferred to walk back and forth, if the weather was inclement, Jane usually persuaded one of the Mounties in the PM's security detail to drive her to the gym. Jane found that taxis could take longer. Some taxi drivers had limited knowledge of the geography of Ottawa and had to constantly phone their dispatcher for directions. She smiled at this phenomenon—Ottawa, the only capital city where taxis get lost. A tourist attraction perhaps, she thought.

Jane had to pay close attention to the state of the sidewalks as she walked home after exercising. There were patches of ice in her way, a result of the melting of pockets of snow in the warm April sun. It was still too early for the puddles to be liquid. Right opposite the Alexandra Bridge, she heard someone shout "Watch out!" As she turned to look, an SUV was mounting the sidewalk at an accelerating speed. She remembered no more.

The car drove away, turning around at the bridge in front of some sedate commuter cars. The SUV tore across the bridge and parked in the parking lot of the Museum of Civilization. Immediately the driver got out and jumped into the passenger side of a BMW compact car. They drove off into the countryside, eventually circling back to the public parking at the airport. The BMW driver immediately got in line for the hourly flight to Toronto. The driver of the SUV was almost immediately on a flight to Montreal. It seemed a well-rehearsed sortie, an assassination planned and executed by professionals.

It was almost three hours later that the police found the SUV, and then only because Avis Car Rental reported it missing. It took a week before the airport police found the missing BMW in the parkade at the airport.

* * *

For a while, Arthur did not think he could cope with the tragedy. The initial shock did not dissipate. It just got augmented by anxiety, anger, fear and, in light of the happenings since the Americans hacked into the Canadian information system, trepidations. The RCMP was doing its best and, in the interests of time, coordinating with the Ottawa Regional Police. No one could believe that the collision was more than just a crazy hit-and-run incident. Assassinations did not happen in Canada except in and between urban gangs.

Arthur let Rose and Stephen take over his schedule in Ottawa. Angie joined him quickly after he had called with the news. She looked after the home fires as it were, and Arthur pulled rank with the Principal of Queen's to ensure that Angie was given a legitimate leave of absence. She was doubtful at this time if she would ever go back.

Stephen drafted the necessary press releases including the one sent first to the Cabinet and then to the caucus and press. It announced that Mario, the deputy prime minister, would be acting prime minister for at least two weeks if not longer. Arthur would soon be leaving for Victoria with Angie.

Vera, in Victoria with his older daughter, Melanie, was a godsend. She met with the undertaker and made the arrangements with the Anglican Cathedral on Quadra Street. The RCMP insisted on playing a key role in ensuring security in both Ottawa and Victoria, including seating arrangements in the Cathedral. Vera also liaised with the Governor General's staff. There was some question that one of the senior royalty might attend the funeral as well as a senior member of the British Cabinet. Barry Evans and his wife might attend too. The list went on. Jason Broadfoot took over temporarily as Chief of Staff in Arthur's office so that Stephen could handle arrangements in Ottawa and in Victoria. Stephen set up a coordinating body comprising Vera, Gerald, Jason (to keep Mario informed) and representatives of the Governor General and the Party. He insisted that he was in charge. Arthur had to sign off on a widely distributed memorandum on organization; every cook wanted to be bottle washer too.

Arthur found it sickening to take phone calls from world leaders.

At least he developed a short script to read that kept the calls brief. When he and Angie, with Gerald and some RCMP colleagues, left for Victoria, five days after Jane's death, there were some glitches as people tried to track him down. Now he really regretted that he and Jane had not bought a house in Victoria, as the two daughters and he must share a small two-bedroom flat in downtown Victoria. He didn't really care what happened to Gerald and his friends. They could find a place to live and personnel to ensure some level of safety.

It did not take long before Vera realised that the Cathedral would not hold the mass of dignitaries who said they might attend. She arranged national coverage of the service with the CBC, but not any telecast of the funeral procession. A private interment was requested by Arthur. The Roman Catholic Cathedral and the First United Church downtown both volunteered their buildings for a relay of the telecast. These sorts of details were beyond Arthur's ken at this time.

The British Press, notably the *Times*, and the *Australian* too, carried a short front-page item on "PM's wife death rumoured suspicious" with an inference that both Jane and Arthur had been mixing with bad company. They pointedly rejected this inference in a one-inch column on its inside pages. Arthur asked Gerald in a morning phone call if he knew about these rumours; Gerald replied that they received three to four such rumours weekly. Stephen said he would get hold of the Commissioner of the RCMP and his deputy for the Pacific Region. Using the maxim, who benefits, Arthur could only think that Anne might but he rejected that idea. It was too implausible although it could make some good press copy. He wondered whether the Americans were somehow involved. Had Jane been indiscreet? He thought the whole hacking incidents were well contained within his inner circle of Cabinet colleagues and senior PMO staff. This was not the time for speculation.

Somewhat unusually, Jane had written a draft of some preferences for her funeral service. It reflected her sense of liturgical traditions, her love of Gregorian chant and her passion for stirring music. She requested the service from the Book of Common Prayer, the Cranmer version not the Canadian medley penned in the early twentieth century. She requested that the service include a female contralto to sing "I know that my Redeemer liveth" from Handel's Messiah. And she wanted a cellist to play the first movement of Elgar's Concerto for Cello. She requested a service at the Cathedral in Victoria because she had full confidence in the Music Director as well as the Dean. This was a rare phenomenon for Anglican congregations.

Arthur, his two daughters and two cousins, as well as Jane's Aunty Flo and Uncle Edmund, all entered the nave together as the congregation stood. The Bishop of British Columbia gave the eulogy. On the way out, Arthur and family stood on the bottom steps of the Cathedral and thanked the guests. The Governor General's staff provided exemplary help. No royals came but the Queen penned her condolences in a hand-written note. Premiers and party leaders all turned out en masse. Roughly half way through the parade, Arthur and his girls backed away and got into a limousine provided by the Party. They were anxious to return to their flat.

Arthur went to bed. He took a stiff brandy as well as some sleeping tablets. All he really wanted was sleep and the chance to wake up from this nightmare.

* * *

Melanie and Angie flew back to Ottawa with Arthur, on Gerald's advice, to avoid crowds of well wishers. They took a CFB Esquimalt helicopter to Vancouver Airport where they could board, at the last moment, some business class seats relatively unnoticed. It was also a direct flight to Ottawa. Arthur was glad to have his daughters' company. They too were grieving. On touchdown, Arthur suggested they have a long talk about Jane's death. It was early evening on arrival back east, so they promised each other a chat the following day. Arthur called Rose, who willingly contacted Mario and the rest of the Cabinet to advise that Arthur would ease back into his official duties the following week. Arthur had the false notion that trying to re-establish a normal routine might help him manage his grief and anger.

Arthur and girls drove to Kingsmere, Mackenzie King's summer home in Gatineau Park. They chanced a stroll in the gardens to avoid precise location. They had realised that their whereabouts were monitored by a locator attached to their car. Arthur actually felt somewhat reassured by the potential pressure of the Mounties.

Melanie reminisced about happy family times—Christmases in Victoria, springs in Parksville, summer holidays plus their many hikes around Prince Edward County in Ontario. She was in tears throughout as was Arthur. Arthur told them about the plans that he and Jane had to retire from public service by this fall and set up a home and small office in Victoria. He imagined he could consult privately with provincial and federal officials and keep busy with those forays east while he worked on his autobiography.

Melanie had only a vague idea of Arthur's childhood. As happens all too often in families, her parents glossed over their early years to focus on their positive life lessons.. Angie wanted, rather she demanded, the details of Arthur's early years, now that she would never have the chance to have the same conversation with her mother.

Arthur described how his two teacher parents used home life to enhance his education and to grade his performance. They were dominating and domineering. As an only child, he had no one to share the criticism. His solution was to tell them the bare minimum and, in later years, to seek solace with school friends and with Jane. He disliked lying. He could easily be found out by either parent. He preferred to tell them some of the whole truth and, since he was successful in school, they were more or less content with his behaviour.

He admitted to Melanie that this strategy of massaging the truth was excellent practice for politics. He could be positive with some, beguilingly frank with others, funny with kids and teens, and, while not avoiding important political, social and economic affairs, he could draw a convenient line between telling the whole truth and sharing only fragments.

Jane had known all about Arthur's past and his proclivity for secrets. She knew how to prise much out of Arthur. He never let go of all of the truth. His affair with Anne was a case in point.

Melanie blurted out her opinions for her Dad in typically brusque fashion. "Resign and retire, Dad," she asserted. "What if Mum was deliberately run down? You might well be next. Out of office, no one will care about you politically-wise."

"Horrible word," exclaimed Arthur, reminding himself of his late father.

"Please, Dad," Melanie pleaded.

"What does your sister think, Mel?" he wondered.

"She agrees with me, Dad."

Silence ensued. "Your opinions and those of Angie are most important to me," Arthur admitted. "I'll have to plan my exit carefully. Another six- months at the max I think," promised Arthur.

* * *

Mark Lofthouse phoned Gerald. It was the week of Arthur's return.

"No more Jane Jones, eh?

Gerald waited a moment before replying, "No more Jane Jones. Our workload will plummet."

Mark replied, "Always ready to help Gerald" and hung up.

Chapter Fourteen: Preparing to Leave

Arthur spent much of the spring and summer supervising the change of leadership to come and also the plans for the party convention in the fall. The convention would combine policy proposals from the candidates, some from the provincial constituencies and some from the debates among candidates. He was determined not to let the CBC, CTV or Global decide how many and which of the candidates would debate. By June, he had agreement from the declared candidates that only the top four in the polls on September 1 would be allowed to participate. Each had roughly ten weeks to get into the top four, although of course some fringe candidates would protest. It effectively excluded some big names who could not decide whether to enter the race or not.

Mario, at Arthur's request, took over as chair of some key Cabinet committees. No one thought Mario had appeal to run as party leader, but he was competent on administrative affairs, knew he should not run, and was influential in Quebec, especially East Montreal. It was a comfortable decision for Arthur. Arthur limited his interests to foreign affairs, the economy and Treasury Board. They had always been his main focus anyway.

Under Stephen's direction, the public service was given some scope to prepare briefing books even though no government would change. They anticipated, probably correctly, that a new PM would want to shuffle the Cabinet and some new members might be unaware of the contexts within in which the Cabinet operated.

Arthur saw little of Anne during these months. Both felt that discretion was essential, although both yearned for each other. Arthur discovered over time that he could be devoted to two women, albeit one who was now dead. He figured he could divide the whole of his brain into discrete segments, including ones for the two women in his life.

The party convention was to be held at the Royal York Hotel in Toronto, largely on the grounds that the hotel was experienced in hosting such events and Toronto was conveniently placed for airline journeys. Arthur toyed with the idea of having everyone meet at the Empress Hotel in Victoria, but everyone close to his thinking protested vigorously due to the costs of travel. Most party members would not attend, wherever the convention would be held. They would be online for preferential balloting. The winner needed to get 50% + one votes of voting members to win the contest.

Arthur spent every weekend in Victoria largely to be close to his two daughters who both obtained summer jobs at home. He sometimes caught a Friday morning plane out of Ottawa and spent a few luxurious hours with Anne at her home in North Burnaby. It became a pleasant routine, soon to be disrupted by the pending convention. Anne was a delegate so they could probably snatch some hours together at night without attracting any publicity.

Arthur always liked party conventions, as had Jane. They both found it refreshing to meet like-minded people, and they enjoyed partying as well as debating. In the early years, when both were party activists, they would try to get delegate status from their Victoria riding. In fairness to other loyal activists, they occasionally took turns to attend. The main problem was the cost of transport and accommodation, unless the convention was in Vancouver which was the case for most BC conventions. In later years, when the girls were a bit older, Jane left them at home with her mother, instead of dragging them to different Canadian cities to see the sights with one or the other of the parents.

Arthur really enjoyed the networking and the range of characters who dedicated themselves to party events. Some were pleased to meet or renew acquaintances. Others looked at their watches or over his shoulder so they could move on to more famous people. Arthur never forgot their names when he started to acquire power and patronage.

It took only a few years for Arthur to realise that party

conventions, even those ostensibly for policy formulation and renewal, were really not about policies. They were about networking and enjoying the company of friends. Good food and wine were essential parts of these trips out of town. The people met this way were later to prove indispensable to Arthur when he began his campaigns for BC Member of Legislative Assembly, for Member of Parliament and for Prime Minister. He could also practice his colloquial French at national conventions.

So Arthur was actually looking forward to the convention, during which he would make a farewell address to the nation as well as to the party delegates. He secured time with the CBC for complete coverage of his speech. And, over the summer, Arthur kept notes on topics that he might include or not. Again he felt how much he missed Jane's ideas and guidance. He also realised that he had made one mistake. He was competing for air time with the Toronto Blue Jays at the end of their baseball season!

* * *

Arthur asked Gerald, his chief personal security officer, to coordinate security with the Toronto Metropolitan Police Force (TMPF) and with Jimmy Evans, the party's "point man" on local arrangements. The next he heard about security was that Gerald was chairing a coordinating committee consisting of representatives of the RCMP, the TMPF, the Party, Pinkerton's private security and, incredibly, the CIA.

Arthur immediately scolded Gerald on the scale of the security and the inclusion of the CIA. Gerald had lots of ready responses, expecting criticism from both Arthur and the party leaders. "There is still some suspicion about the circumstances of your wife's death, sir," Gerald asserted. "And we don't know the scale of any protests yet. It wouldn't be a G-20 scale protest, we are sure, but it could be the size of the Vancouver hockey riots of 2011 or even the Tottenham riots in London of the same year. We need to plan for the worst."

"Gerald, are you suggesting that Jane was assassinated? I know some British press ran early stories to that effect, but the supermarket press didn't think that either Jane or I was sexy or well-known enough to put us on page 1 or page anywhere." Arthur went on, "In politics, Gerald, hypothetical stories end up being believed by opponents and their supporters just because they may hate the personality or the party under scrutiny. Planting a seed can bring forth a weed as fast as a flower.

"You and I have reviewed the evidence on Jane's death. No one had a motive. The crazy driver got clean away, we think by foot, into the Museum of Civilization and later by cab into the Gatineau hillside.

"And why the Americans? Arthur went on.

Gerald readily replied, "We have an agreement with the Americans signed during the Harper Administration that both countries would collaborate and coordinate on security matters. I clarified the status of this agreement with the Department of Foreign Affairs and International Trade, and my colleagues in the CIA confirmed my arrangements. There is a continuing fear that some terrorist organization may have masterminded your wife's death. We can't rule it out."

"You have little understanding of politics, Gerald," replied Arthur. "With respect, I want you to resign as chair of the coordinating committee but stay a member for liaison purposes. I will ask Jimmy Evans to chair and the Toronto Police Chief to act as deputy chair. We need to put the local experts in charge. Poppycock to the terrorist language!"

"You are showing a lack of confidence in me, Prime Minister, and in the RCMP detail here to protect you. I may have to consider my position and will review your comments with my Commissioner."

"Very well, Gerald. Do what you must. Just remember, the Commissioner is appointed by the Privy Council; that is, me. I think he will support my position to avoid alarmist postures over a convention of 500 people. If things change, the TMPF can bring in extra help."

Arthur needed some fresh air and a break from his office routine. After explaining his argument to Stephen, Arthur went for a walk along the Rideau Canal using some back routes to reach the canal unnoticed. He wished he had gone to see Anne, but remembered that she was spending most of the summer in Burnaby largely to avoid the humidity that hung over Southern Ontario and Southern Quebec during July and August.

Apart from the brief argument with Gerald, the summer had been quite placid since Jane's funeral. It was a welcome relief, but Arthur had some concerns. In his experience, politics was never placid. Constant change interspersed with a potential or actual crisis was the norm. There was never a stable equilibrium. Events always interceded. Some were on foreign territory, but the majority occurred due to vigilant press investigations at home reporting yet another bureaucratic or political mistake. Arthur's expertise lay in part in anticipating these events and adapting quickly to their political significance. As Arthur strolled along the canal embankment, he recalled his Austrian economics. Social and economic events were too complex to sustain equilibrium.

Arthur noticed that his RCMP tail was catching up with his own slow pace. There must be a message; Arthur deliberately refused to take his cell phone when he went for a walk. The Mountie caught up with Arthur and, holding out a phone, indicated that Stephen was looking for him.

"Come back to your office quickly, Arthur," was Stephen's tense message. "Some new political happenings for you" He ended with a laugh. Both Stephen and Arthur enjoyed the ironies in political life.

* * *

"We've had two people declare their candidacies for the leadership, almost simultaneously," was Stephen's first comments when they were alone in the PM's office. The Minister of Finance, as anticipated, declared in his constituency office in Toronto Rosedale, and it was hard for all of the media and party members to squeeze into the space. John liked to cause congestion, convinced that a big crowd overflowing its meeting place was an indication of approval. Arthur thought it was a little childish—the media know the game. John had been sounding out party leaders across the country for some time. He was generally admired as a sound person, albeit a bit slow for widespread popularity. He knew Bay Street well, as his own background had been with the Toronto Dominion Bank, handling both investments and retail activities.

Arthur had known John for many years and had come to rely on his wisdom in the finance portfolio. They shared a frugal approach to the government's finances. More important, they trusted each other, ever since the time when both had been elected to Parliament in the same year.

That same day another candidate declared in Halifax. Andy Murray, Opposition leader in the Nova Scotia Legislature, announced his candidacy in the Lord Nelson Hotel. Andy was well known "down east" and had kept the Party alive during its lean years. The press release declared that Andy was 65, but friends and enemies knew that Andy always cheated on his age. Arthur guessed that Andy was at least ten years older than he, and Arthur was 59. It didn't seem rational for Andy to think he could win either the leadership or the country. He was no stupid man either, thought Arthur. There is another game he wants to play, something more complicated than some pork barrel for Halifax.

During the remainder of June and into July, more candidates declared. Brian Jones, an up-and-coming MP from Vancouver Mountain, was the most significant in Stephen's view. He had successfully defeated a long-time incumbent in the last election and his image as a "heartthrob" with the ladies was regularly referred to as qualification. Arthur liked him because he could speak in complete sentences, never using an "um" or a "like" or "Mr. Speaker" as he gathered his thoughts. Arthur took this as an indication of an agile mind. But he was very young and inexperienced for the old-time party leaders. Probably he is after a Cabinet seat if he shows well in the campaigns and vote, Stephen announced.

In mid-August, Arthur was shocked and hurt. To the group of six or seven candidates was added the sole Quebecer: Mario. He had phoned Arthur and tried to explain his decision.

"There are no French candidates in the race," was Mario's main point. "We have no working class candidates unless you count the two MPs from Northern Ontario. We always try to rotate the leadership between English and French Canada and it is our time now. I have been a successful deputy prime minister, especially in the last months!"

Arthur thought these statements were a catalogue of self-renewing excuses, as if Mario were a small boy caught drinking beer behind a garden shed.

"Well, Mario," said Arthur. "I am surprised. I gave you extra responsibilities in Cabinet precisely because you were not running for leader. You've been a loyal colleague from Quebec. We'll just have to deal with your immediate resignation from Cabinet. Fortunately, we will only lose you and John at this time, and no other Cabinet colleagues seem prepared to run. I expect you know that. Good luck, Mario. I wish you well."

Arthur placed the phone down delicately. He was amused at how some listening and talking could lead him to offer good wishes to Mario, while he stuffed the angry bits of his reaction in a different mental place. He already knew that Gilles would make the best acting replacement. Parliament would not be sitting until after the party convention so the duties of House Leader would be significantly reduced. Gilles was also a trusted friend and ally. Arthur was not convinced that Cabinet confidences would now be easily kept by Mario.

* * *

President Evans sat at his desk in the Oval Office sporting his usual plastic smile, but his eyes betrayed some inner anger. Beryl Rossini and Fred Riggs sat on hard-backed chairs in front of the desk. They had requested a meeting with the President in advance of the National Security Council meeting that August week. They needed to include an emergency item for discussion; that is, if the President preferred a group discussion before he made any decision. Barry loved options and Beryl indulged his predilections.

The issue, Beryl explained, was "What to do about Canada?" She recounted how they had both visited Ottawa and Barry had apologised before a joint session of both Houses of Parliament for the blunder of some Pentagon staff in hacking into the computers of the Prime Minister's Office and those with which it was networked. On the advice of the CIA and, it was understood, the RCMP, they had put a "tail" on Jane Jones as she seemed quite unpredictable and hostile to security forces. They traced her to Cortes Island, in British

Columbia, by hacking into her regular telephone lines at the Prime Minister's home and discovering that she had booked a flight to Victoria and then drove to Campbell River to catch a ferry to the Island. Deeper investigations at the three car rental counters at the Victoria airport revealed only one rental that particular evening to a Jane Smith (not Jones)! They had heard about her relationship with the former Premier, now living on Cortes Island. It was apparently strictly platonic, and sources thought that Dave might have preferred the male gender. Regardless, Dave was a long-time friend and mentor of both the Jones'.

Barry was beginning to get restless. "Cut to the chase, Beryl," he blurted out. "I'm too busy for gossip of any kind, even though Jane is or was one sexy bitch."

"OK, OK," Beryl replied. "Anyway, our men persuaded Dave to reveal what he knew about Jane's involvement with security. He eventually told us that it was Arthur and his inner circle who had sent the virus to the Pentagon, apparently just to see where the hacking into their system had originated."

"Yeah"?Barry interrupted. "This was simply exploratory? Pull the other leg, Beryl, or should I say Dave?"

"I thought the same," said Fred, finally opening his mouth. "Arthur Jones may be the Prime Minister of a medium-sized ally, but he is a sneaky bugger in our view. He always seems to be backing our public pronouncements and then taking divergent paths."

"Go on, Beryl," Barry said loudly.

Beryl allowed as how difficult it normally was to keep tabs on Jane or Arthur as they kept using new cell phones and calling from walks around buildings. "She simply seems to have forgotten to use a cell phone to book airline tickets."

"So what about the hoax? Did the Canadians do that?"

"We don't think so," Beryl replied. "It doesn't smell like the Canadians. They may be devious but they aren't very sneaky on international matters."

"What do you advise" Barry asked the two of them. "Arthur will be out of office soon and out of our hair. What about his poor wife? Any new information on how she died?"

Beryl bit her lip, visibly. "We are still following that. The RCMP is of no help. They like to blame the commuter traffic and the local cops for some cold trails. Our man Lofthouse, in charge of the investigations in Ottawa for us, swears it might have been an assassination. But we don't know by whom unless we took a gamble and blamed the Israelis or the Palestinians, neither of whom have reasons to keep Jane silent."

Barry stopped the conversation and held up his hand. "This need not go to the NSC. It doesn't need major discussion or implementation. We need the CIA to follow the trail in Canada, perhaps with more resources located in our Ottawa Embassy or Vancouver Consulate. Will you stay in charge, Beryl, and keep us informed of any new developments? I think we need to follow up the information provided by Lofthouse, but that is all for now."

Beryl and Fred left. Barry thought for a minute or two. "Get me the Israeli Prime Minister, please," he spoke into the intercom.

* * *

Arthur spent the balance of the summer looking after major portfolios with the help of the ministers of state promoted on an acting basis into the portfolios left by John and Mario. Gilles could handle the few issues involving the parliamentary recall as well as deputizing for Mario on Cabinet and Cabinet committees. Arthur himself kept watch over the finance portfolio with the acting minister, the minister of state for financial institutions. Both relied too much, thought Arthur, on the belaboured machinations of the Bank of Canada. Arthur couldn't understand the blinkered mindset of finance people who, while recognizing some of the imperfections of concepts like Gross Domestic Product, still used a crude utilitarian calculus to evaluate policy options. He did not bother to fight them. That battle was lost many decades ago. He would solve the minor problems and leave "the biggies" for his successor. He did note how slavishly devoted to John were the personal staff left in his office. He found that affection reassuring as he shared it too.

Arthur's weekends in Burnaby were sheer bliss. He used to feel guilt and remorse together when he remembered Jane, often in the middle of passionate love with Anne. Sometimes the thoughts aborted his erection. Other times they enhanced it. Anne recognized these phenomena. She was an experienced lover and alternately passionate or cuddly when needed. She could always tempt him back to an explosive erection within a moment or two of oral sex. And he could always remind her of her deep desires and love for Arthur. When the passion was finally exhausted, they talked of the coming convention. Anne was to play an MC role during one of the sessions. Which session was yet to be decided.

* * *

Arthur was sitting in his suite at the Royal York. It was traditionally appointed, which Arthur liked. He knew exactly where Stephen and Anne were located. Gerald never liked to share those details, thinking that "close by" would satisfy the Prime Minister. Arthur had arranged for three TVs in his room: one focussed on the convention stage and the others hooked up to whatever stations Arthur wanted at any time.

At 8 pm, each of the four major candidates was given five minutes to outline their policy planks, in advance of the Saturday debate and the Sunday vote. After a tribute to Arthur at 8:30 pm—a slick presentation put together by communication staff in his office— Arthur would speak from 9 pm to 10 pm. Arthur loved to be admired but hated the format of media "experts" who seemed to believe that baby pictures foretold the development of the grown man. On the Friday night in question, Arthur settled down in front of the TVs, his speech in his inside jacket pocket, the TV remote in his left hand and a scotch and soda in this right. He felt comfortable and amused.

The speeches began in a predictable way. John Bradshaw, Arthur's loyal friend, began by emphasizing "the steady ship of state" theme and ending with promises of a newer and better economic prosperity for Canada's new eco-conscious society. Brian Jones promised a new, reinvigorated party and government for the next generations of unborn children and grandchildren. B- grade thought Arthur. John had been his usual A-. Now it was onto Andy Murray who talked about the party as a party of people from all regions and inclusive of origins, class and gender. He would tweak these priorities by adding a new approach to defence policies with the major issue being border security on all four frontiers and a new quick strike navy for the three oceans and the Great Lakes. More shipbuilding thought Arthur. Here is another politician talking in codes. Just a B for him in Arthur's view.

Mario began by repeating the kinds of arguments he used on Arthur when he announced his candidacy. The party had a forgotten tradition of alternating English and French leaders, and he had firsthand experience at running both departments of government and, for the last few months, much of the operations. He then enunciated a startling set of assertions and plans. Arthur had apparently left too much of foreign policy to be dictated by the US. He had been temperamental about the computer hacking incident which needed the US President's visit to placate. Jane's death was perhaps an assassination that Arthur, in his situation, could not appreciate or resolve. He, Mario, could establish a full judicially chaired committee of investigation into the hacking, the assassination and the PMO operations between the two. Mario implied that he knew the truth, the whole truth, not just the parts of the truth that Arthur had made public. It was a well-presented speech—perhaps an A—but Arthur could only see the implications and dangers of Mario's comments. Mario must have used his time in the last few months to go through some of the files in the PMO. He could not have been privy to the details of the Israeli liaison, but he could have known about the virus mission that ended up in the Pentagon. Arthur thought his private life with Jane and his public life in Ottawa would be destroyed by a commission. Mario would make sure that his friends would staff and indeed chair the body he would establish.

Now Arthur had to go downstairs to the convention and redo his farewell speech almost immediately. He resolved to tell some of the truth, if only to calm his own nerves.

*　*　*

Arthur received a rousing welcome from the delegates. He must have shaken one hundred hands as he entered from the back of the hall into a crowd of some three hundred cheering loyalists. He felt energized. Now he could talk.

"I speak to you as your party leader and Prime Minister for the last 8 years. During my time in office, Canada has sailed through some choppy waters into well navigated and peaceful seas."

He provided a few statistics to emphasize his leadership as one of a learned professor of the people. He then went off script, and he knew the reporters would be mad at him for doing so. He needed to respond to Mario.

"Mario has alluded to some difficult times for me personally and for the government, all of which took place within the last year. We have carried on government with prosperity and frugality, and implemented more of our mandate for climate control, dental care for children and in-home support for seniors. We have developed policies to help all of the population, not just one region or one segment of our communities.

"We were challenged by the computer hacking incident but, with the help of the Americans and experts from other countries, our in-house people restored our firewalls. We know, of course, that the hackers came from the US and abused their positions within the American government. The Americans suspect that the hoax about Zimbabwe and their own computer incidents were caused by others within the US. We are happy to share the conclusions of the American government with all Canadians. We think, as do many Americans in and out of government, that their country may harbour some anarchists who may have undue access to their government. We also think that there are good reasons to suspect foul play from these people with regard to the death of Jane." He paused and wiped his eyes. He was no good at crocodile tears. These were the genuine article.

Arthur seized the podium with both hands. "The RCMP will hound down the anarchists, and we will fly them to Baffin Island when we find them, regardless of citizenship. We cannot let Americans or other nationals destroy our peaceable kingdom as an experiment or conspire to rid the world of people like Jane because of documented distaste for American foreign policy.

"There is no place on Baffin Island yet to house these criminals. I'm sure the next Prime Minister will find a way to punish the intruders. Before I leave office in a month's time, I want to inform the American government that their citizens will need to take a furlough (Arthur used his Southern accent for that word) from Canada. The next Prime Minister, one of these four good people, will then have the dubious pleasure of lifting the barriers. I will not leave office as a 'do nothing' Prime Minister, nor as a Prime Minister that could not prevent invasions of our territory and security."

With that, all the lights in the room went out. Some people screamed, others gasped, noises came from scraping chairs and tables. The lights were back on within three or four minutes, but there was no one on the stage. Arthur had disappeared. The chair of the session stumbled to the podium. She announced that an explanation for the power outage and for the missing Prime Minister would be sought immediately and communicated to all. "Please exit the hall as soon as possible." They did.

Chapter Fifteen: The End or Not the End?

He gradually opened his eyes. It was a hotel room, he thought, but it could have been a dormitory residence room with a single bed. It had one small desk, metal and scraped. It had no closet. Slowly he moved to the window. The shutters had been nailed shut. The curtains were actually quite tasteful. They must have come from Value Village after a funeral time donation from relatives of the deceased.

No pictures on the wall. A small sink faced him. While his head throbbed, he took some reasonably cold water from the tap. Since there was no obvious place to relieve himself, he urinated in the sink and tried to wash it down with some warm water and hand soap. He staggered back to bed. He could not remember anything about how he got to this place. He did remember that he had been speaking at the convention and then nothing else. Was he still in Toronto? Was he still (just) the Prime Minister? Suddenly, he knew he had been kidnapped—the locked door, the nailed shutters, the sparse furnishings, the bare light bulb. Was this limbo? He smiled at his own joke, but it hurt his head. He decided to try to get some more sleep.

A key scraping to fit into the door lock woke him. In walked Gerald and Mark Lofthouse, with Lofthouse dangling a key chain.

"I see you are awake," said Mark. "We drugged you with a specified dose to last until about now. We are quite good at injection, aren't we Gerald?"

"Where am I?" asked Arthur with a raspy voice. "And can I have some water?"

Gerald fished inside his outer coat pockets and came up with a

108

half-full bottle of water. "This will have to do," he grunted. "And we are actually in an immigration detention centre in Niagara Falls, New York, where US Homeland Security detain illegal immigrants from Canada. Not too far from home." He smirked as if that news would please Arthur.

Lofthouse intervened, "We believe you ordered the hoax on the US government, with the help of the Israelis. The Israelis deny any knowledge, of course, but we have Canadian sources who can vouch for this incredibly stupid joke."

There was a moment's silence. Arthur wondered who on earth would have given the Americans this news. He also felt reassured that the Israelis had kept their promise to remain silent. They were a reliable ally.

"We will get you something to eat," said Gerald.

Arthur replied, "Gerald, what the hell are you doing, collaborating to kidnap and drug your Prime Minister? Is this your idea of security?"

"We collaborate and cooperate with the Americans all the time," Gerald replied. "The RCMP, CSIS, CIA and US border security work as a team."

"A practical joke is not a border security issue," Arthur allowed. "What happens now?"

Lofthouse was the first to answer. "We suspect your government of destroying our computer resources in the Pentagon by planting a virus there. We don't know how you did it. But since you were irresponsible enough to play a hoax on our country, you are the next best bet to be the source of the viral invasion. We need to treat that incident like 9/11. It was a cold-blooded invasion. We will probably take you to Guantanamo Bay for further questioning."

"So why did you stop here at Niagara Falls?" replied Arthur.

"That's simple," said Lofthouse. "We came by car, and it is easier to put a drugged person in a car and disguise the fact, than to load them onto a US military aircraft on a Toronto runway."

"I'll be back in five minutes," said Gerald. "Do you need anything, Mark?"

"Nope." was the terse reply.

They did not speak until Gerald returned. Mark sat at the end of Arthur's bed and amused himself by unloading and then reloading his handgun. Arthur could feel his own anger mounting at this display, indeed at the whole incident. He also knew that it was wiser to stay silent and try to think through the alternatives.

Gerald returned with a large plastic-wrapped bread roll that had a wisp of lettuce hanging out of one side. It was a typical vending machine roll—stale but almost $10. Gerald smiled and said, "The roll is on me, Arthur. I'll expense it when I return to Ottawa."

By now, Arthur believed that Mark and Gerald were both crazy. Their actions were preposterous, but he realised that the rule of law was a forgotten code of conduct for police and security forces, at least those involved with international affairs.

* * *

Arthur was taken through a side door in the corridor outside his room and straight onto the tarmac of the small airport. There were just the three of them. They walked across the tarmac to a US military helicopter that must have been able to seat a dozen or more. A pilot was in the cabin probably formalizing his flight plan. He had no co-pilot with him.

Inside, Arthur was led to a seat that was only about six feet behind the pilot's seat. Gerald sat next to him with Mark across the aisle, trying not to look smug.

Arthur decided to speak up. "Have you the President's permission to take us to Guantanamo? Am I listed as a criminal in your files?" he asked Mark.

Mark said that those were silly questions. He had full discretion to handle this situation although he doubted that the President knew right now what was planned. They'd get Arthur off the continental US first and tell Rossini and Riggs second. They could deal with the President.

Arthur did not give up. "If you take me to Guantanamo, your secret won't last long. The rest of the world will condemn the US. Canada will severely cut diplomatic ties if not more."

"I think not, Mr. Prime Minister," said Mark. "America is a sovereign country, and if you instigated the computer virus invasion, the situation will be viewed like 9/11 or Pearl Harbour."

"But what if I did not inspire that so-called invasion? You and the CIA hierarchy will find yourselves discharged and the President asked to apologise to Ottawa for a second time."

"Wait here," Mark declared. "I'm calling Rossini right now. Gerald can keep an eye on you. I'll be back in five or less." With that he hopped out of the helicopter and disappeared across the tarmac into the one-level cinder block "holding tank" for illegal immigrants.

Gerald got up and strode to the pilot, placing his pistol against the pilot's head. "I want you to take off right now before Mark comes back. Head for Ottawa as fast as possible. Cross into Canada quickly. If you resist, I'll blow your head off and pilot the helicopter myself. I'm a qualified pilot." That was only partly true. He had lots of flying hours as an amateur pilot, but none in a helicopter of this size.

The pilot started the helicopter, and the engine responded quickly. He did not need the permission of any tower to take off. Once up fifty feet he headed due north, with Gerald still holding the gun to his head.

"Good on ya, Gerald," said Arthur, still in his seat. "Thanks boss," Gerald replied.

Gerald directed the pilot to land at Hamilton Airport, a large airport with relatively few flights and passengers. He told the Prime Minister that he would call his Commissioner in Ottawa and tell him that the two of them plus the pilot and helicopter would soon be at Hamilton. He'd then ask the pilot to return to Niagara Falls immediately. The pilot was a party to those comments and decided to keep quiet. It was too interesting a day to spoil right now.

The landing and deplaning went smoothly, and the helicopter was back in the air before Gerald and Arthur had walked the 800 metres to the terminal building.

Gerald rented a car, a small Kia Soul, and they drove to Billy Bishop Airport on Toronto Island to catch a small Bombardier plane to Ottawa. Some passengers recognized Arthur but did not accost him. Probably all of them knew he had disappeared, but felt nonplussed to see him alive in the company of a tall blonde man with an officious air.

Unfortunately a huge crowd awaited them at the Ottawa Airport. Someone in the RCMP must have leaked the news after Gerald called to say they were returning.

Before they landed, Arthur asked Gerald why he had collaborated over his kidnapping, drugging and confinement. Gerald said first, "That's what I'm paid to do. Look after you. I knew I'd get you out of the fix more easily by cooperating with the CIA than if they had orchestrated a kidnapping by themselves. Outside the US they have difficulty in organising a church social."

Arthur smiled. Gerald allowed as now they needed to avoid the media scrum at the airport. Arthur borrowed Gerald's phone and called Stephen so that he could organise a private deplaning with RCMP protection. The plane could taxi onto a spot off runway while the logistics were worked out.

* * *

At the Prime Minister's residence, Gerald and Arthur enjoyed a celebratory scotch and soda.

"It was great," said Gerald. He pulled out his pistol and shot Arthur in his kneecap. "I promised President Evans that I'd do that."

Arthur now knew that his retirement would contain his revenge....

Cast of Characters

Andy Murray	Leadership hopeful
Angela/Angie Jones	Daughter of PM
Anne Barnaby	Member of Parliament for /PM's lover
Arthur Jones	Prime Minister of Canada
Barry Evans	President of the United States
Ben Levitt	US VP
Bert Condon	Leader of the Third Party
Beryl Rossini	US Secretary of State
Brian Eddy	RCMP
Brian Jones	MP from Vancouver Mountain/Leadership hopeful
Carol	"chief media person" (Director of Communications, PMO)
Dave Bond	Friend on Cortes Island/Former BC Premier
David	Minister of National Security
Debbie Evans	US First Lady
Denise	PM's parliamentary secretary
Edgar	PM of Israel
Elaine	Executive assistant to Arthur Jones
Fred Riggs	Secretary of Defence, US

Cast of Characters (contd.)

Gary Prevost	Chair of House Cttee on Foreign Affairs and Defence
George Conway	Minister of Aboriginal Affairs and Northern Development
Gerald	Head of PM's security detail
Gilbert	RCMP Commissioner
Gilles	House Leader
Gordon	PM's driver
Graham	Clerk of the Privy Council
Jane Jones	Wife of the PM
Jason Broadfoot	PMO official
Jimmy	PM of Australia
Jimmy Evans	"point man" for the party in Toronto
Jimmy	Minister of National Revenue and Natural Resources
Jo Zed	South Africa President
John Bradshaw	Minister of Finance
Katich	Opposition Leader
Louis Blanc	Party Whip
Mario	Deputy Prime Minister
Mark Lofthouse	Director of CIA
Maurice	Leader of 4th party
Melanie Jones	Daughter of PM

Cast of Characters (contd.)

Raj	Minister of Foreign Affairs
Richard	CSIS
Rose	PM's secretary
Sally and Brian Barrymore	Friends of Arthur and Jane Jones
Sam	Foreign policy advisor, US
Stephen	Chief of Staff, PMO
Tasha	Executive assistant to Arthur Jones
Todd Beecham	Director of FBI
Tom	Minister of National Defence
Vera	PM's secretary in constituency office